GOATS GONE WILD 2

RUTH PRICE

ISBN: 0692668799
ISBN-13: 978-0692668795

TABLE OF CONTENTS

ACKNOWLEDGMENTS

All Praise first to the Almighty God who has given me this wonderful opportunity to share my words and stories with the world. Next, I have to thank my family, especially my husband Harold who supports me even when I am being extremely crabby. Further, I have to thank my wonderful friends and associates with Global Grafx Press who support me in every way as a writer. Lastly, I wouldn't be able to do any of this without you, my readers. I hold you in my heart and prayers and hope that you enjoy my books.

CHAPTER ONE

The sound of barking slowly pulled Annie Miller up from the depths of a sound sleep. She opened one eye and frowned, but the din was too loud to be a dream. Something had happened to set their collie off, and it sounded like he was throwing himself against the back door. The dog was snarling as if he'd saw the devil.

Annie groaned, sat up in her bed groggily, and rubbed her eyes. She hated the thought of getting up. The wooden floor of her Daed's old farmhouse was going to feel like a sheet of ice on such a frosty February night. But Ted was going crazy, and that meant that *something* was outside. She could hear him scratching frantically at the back porch door, and whining in frustration.

The peaceful silence just below Annie's bedroom window was suddenly broken by a sudden storm of slavering yips and growls, answered by many others, fainter and farther off. The sound sent a thrill of fear slithering down her spine. *Coyotes —*

in their back yard!

Annie remembered the goats, and spat out an exclamation. She flung off the covers and went running, barefoot, to her Daed's upstairs study. He kept his pistol in the upper drawer of his desk. Annie fumbled along the deskfront in the dark and found the pistol in the drawer. She checked the safety, grabbed the gun in both hands, and went flying down the stairs to the back porch.

The goats were closed up in the barn, but the barn was old, and some of the planking had been warped by rain and cold. There were spots where a dog might dig its way in.

Or a coyote.

"Get back, Ted!" Annie pushed the collie away from the door and peered out. The moon was like a white spotlight shining down on the snowy yard, and to Annie's horror, a half-dozen wolflike shapes flitted back and forth across it. There was a sudden *crash*, and sounds of chaos, from the direction of the chicken house. Annie cursed under her breath.

She pushed Ted aside with her foot, opened the door, and squeezed through it before the collie could follow her out. She stepped to the edge of the porch and squinted, trying to get a fix on the moving shadows.

The slinking shapes froze, and for a split second Annie and the coyotes stared at one another. A low growl rose up from somewhere in the middle of the yard.

Annie lifted the pistol in both hands, flicked the safety off, and squeezed the trigger: *bang bang bang bang.*

The shadows loped to the trees and were swallowed up by the darkness. They were gone long before the echoes of the pistol shots had faded.

Annie stood there, heart pounding. Then she remembered the goats.

She reset the gun safety, went flying across the moonlit yard, opened the barn door, and slammed it shut behind her. She set the gun on the little table beside the door and lit the kerosene lamp.

The does' eyes were like saucers, and they were screaming in terror, mouths wide open. Annie lifted the lantern high overhead, and swept the barn with its light, but to her relief, there was no sign of any coyote inside and there were still three does in the pen. Ginnie, their buggy horse, was moving restlessly in her stall, and rolled her eyes so that the whites shone.

Annie slumped in relief. The instant she was reassured about the animals, the cold gripped her with its icy fingers. Even though her Daed had gas heaters in the barn, they were totally inadequate for a barefoot girl on a winter's night.

She could hear Ted barking his head off inside the house, and her Daed's voice calling from the back porch: "*Annie? Annie, are you all right?*"

"I'm in the barn," she yelled, "I was checking on the goats."

"What were those gunshots?"

"It was me. I was shooting at coyotes!"

"Come back inside the house. I'll check on the animals."

Annie slipped out, closed the door behind her, and ran back to the safety of the house.

Her father was standing at the back door, wrapped in a dark housecoat and bathed in the yellow light of a kerosene lamp. "Annie Miller, what were you doing outside in your nightgown and no shoes!" he marveled. "You'll catch your death out there! Come inside and go back to bed."

"There were six coyotes in the back yard," Annie told him, panting, "maybe more. I think they were after the goats, but the goats are safe. I scared them off."

"I think you scared *me*, too," Mose replied with asperity, "waking me up in the middle of the night with pistol shots!"

"I left the gun on the table in the barn," Annie told him, "and the lamp is still burning."

"Go to bed," Mose told her. "I'll check on the animals. I'll be back in a little while."

He pulled the housecoat tight around him and headed off to the barn. Annie kept vigil at the door and watched as he entered the barn, and then came out. He closed the door, and then performed a quick inspection of the yard with the lantern. Finally he returned, sputtering with the cold.

"Whew! It's an icy night for such goings on!" Mose murmured, and closed the door snugly behind him. "It looks like they took a few of the chickens, but you got two of the coyotes. I don't think the rest will be coming back soon."

He shook his shaggy head of salt-and-pepper hair. "But that makes the third attack in the district this month. Those coyotes are getting out of hand. I'm going to bring it up next Sunday – it looks like the men of this valley need to go on another hunting party!"

Ted barked and pawed at his master's leg. Mose looked down at the dog. "Calm down now, Ted," he murmured, patting the fretting collie, "you're not the mighty hunter that you think."

The dog barked and whined and trotted off at his master's heels as he climbed the stairs up to the study. Annie followed him, lamp in hand.

"If this happens again, Annie," Mose told her, over his shoulder, "I want you to call me instead of running outside with the pistol. "You should know better than to go out into the dark alone with a pack of wild animals in the yard!"

"I had the gun," Annie told him.

"A lone girl can't challenge a pack of coyotes," Mose told her firmly, and turned into the study. He walked to his desk and put the gun back into the drawer.

He looked up at her, and the dim light made his eyes look bigger and darker than usual. "Mind me, Annie, if they come back, you're to get *me* and not the gun!"

"I've been hunting since I was ten," Annie objected, but Mose held up an admonishing finger.

"Don't make me lock it up, Annie Miller," he warned, and she sighed and crossed her arms.

"I promise," she sighed.

Mose pulled his housecoat tighter around him and mumbled disapprovingly all the way back to his bedroom.

"Goingoutsidealoneinthemiddleofthenighttoshootcoyotes. *Humphh!*"

Annie watched him go, and then turned to her own bedroom. She put the lantern down on the nightstand and blew it out, but couldn't keep herself from drifting to the window.

There was no sound and no motion in the moonlit yard below. But Annie scanned the dark trees worriedly. She didn't share her father's confidence.

She knew that sooner or later, the coyotes would come back.

CHAPTER TWO

The next morning, Annie watched from the back porch as her father poured kerosene over the coyote carcasses. She shuddered, and was glad that she hadn't been able to see them the night before. The animals were huge, with bristling grizzled coats, glaring eyes, and monstrous teeth.

Mose stepped back, tossed a lighted match on the dead animals, and returned to the porch.

"Come inside, Annie," he told her, and the fire gleamed in Annie's sober eyes as she turned away.

"Remember," her father commanded, "no skating on the pond and no walking outside without me or some other adult."

Annie pulled her mouth down, but couldn't argue. The coyotes' fangs were still fresh in her mind. She wondered how on earth she was going to get the does through the winter with packs of hunting coyotes roaming the countryside.

"It isn't safe to be out alone with those animals on the prowl. Some of them are half wolf," Mose sighed, as he led the way back to the kitchen. He sat down at the table, and Annie poured him a cup of coffee. "It must be the weather that's making them so bold. It's been so bitter out, I guess they're having trouble finding prey."

Tim appeared at the bottom of the stairs, tucking his shirttails in. He yawned.

"What's the fire out back?" he asked.

His father frowned at him. "If you hadn't slept in this morning, you'd know, Timothy Miller! A pack of coyotes was out there last night! Annie shot two of them."

Tim shrugged and grabbed for a plate of pancakes, and his father slapped his hand. "Prayer first – get your hand away! I'm raising a houseful of heathens! Come and sit down, Annie, and you, Timothy, bow your head, so I can at least pretend that I have pious children!"

Annie wiped her hands on a dish towel and sat down at the table. Mose gave his young son a quelling look, and then closed his eyes – a signal for silent prayer.

When he raised them again, he looked at Tim over the bacon platter. "After you finish eating, Tim, I want you to go out and look around for the chickens, in case there are some that got away. We're missing four of them."

Then he turned to Annie. "Annie, Daniel Gingerich is

coming out this morning to teach you about your goats. He should be here before too long. I want you to listen carefully to what he has to say. Nobody around here knows more about goats than he does."

Annie nodded, but ate her breakfast in glum silence. Every time that she thought those hateful goats couldn't possibly be any more trouble, they found a way to surprise her.

The coyotes had come for them, not the chickens; she was sure of it. That morning, she'd found evidence of what she feared: there were scratch marks and torn earth at a weak spot in the barn wall. The coyotes had tried to dig their way in, and when that hadn't worked, they'd grabbed a few hens instead.

She shook her head. Most of the time, the goats made her so mad that she would gladly have *thrown* them to the coyotes. The little monsters were stupid, bad-tempered and a real burden. But they were also her last chance to show her father that she could be competent and responsible – that she was growing up, a little bit.

Those goats were her ticket to a paying assistant manager's spot at her father's store. That is, if they weren't devoured by marauding animals first.

After breakfast, Annie shrugged into a coat and went out to feed and water the animals. The goats started screaming the instant she opened the barn door. Annie grumbled as she moved about, thinking that she understood now why Daniel Gingerich had been so eager to get away from his job tending such irritating animals.

Annie made sure the does' water was fresh and clean, and gave them their morning allotment of hay, but if she was expecting gratitude, she was quickly disillusioned. Her goats were small – some might almost say cute, with their floppy ears – but they were already showing an irritable nature.

Annie sprinkled hay into the feeding trough, and one of the does tilted its head and politely *crunched* her hand between its teeth.

"*Ow*, you little monster!" Annie howled. She yanked her hand back and had to stick it into her armpit, and stomp around the barn at least three times, before the throbbing started to subside.

And when she calmed down enough to take the does outside for a little exercise in the yard, they all three began trying to butt her.

Annie repressed the urge to kick them away. "Oh, stop it, you little devils!" she yelped. "What's the matter with you?"

"That's not the way to start life with your new goats."

Annie looked up to see that Daniel Gingerich had arrived and was picking his way across the icy yard.

"Oh, I hope they *choke*," Annie muttered savagely. "Look at my hand! And it isn't the first time!"

Daniel looked down, and it seemed to Annie that he was

trying not to laugh.

"It isn't funny, Daniel. It hurts!"

His black hat bobbed up and down. "Yes, goats bite. They're working out who gets to be the boss, and they'll never stop fighting over it."

"Great," Annie muttered.

"Oh, they're not bad-tempered, Annie, not really. You just have to understand how they think. You have to show them that *you're* the boss. Like this." Daniel walked up to one of the does and hooked his toe under her belly. He pushed her away, just hard enough to make her wobble.

"See? Not too hard. You don't want to knock her down. Just hard enough to throw her off balance, to show her that she's not the boss of you. They have to be reminded now and then."

He looked up, and his gaze travelled over the yard to the smoking pile of bones – a charred black pile against the fresh white snow. He wrinkled his nose. "Good grief, what's that?"

"Oh, a pack of coyotes was here last night," Annie told him, and sucked the side of her hand. "They were trying to get these stupid goats! I shot two of them, and the others ran away. But I'm sure they'll be back."

Daniel shook his head and frowned. "They're hitting every farm in the valley," he muttered. "I heard that they got Ruben Miller's dog last week. It was his children's pet, too."

"I don't know how I'm going to get these does through the winter uneaten," Annie growled, staring down at them.

"They should be all right in the barn," Daniel replied, looking at it. "Just make sure there are no holes where the coyotes might get in. And it might be smart not to let the goats wander beyond the yard, when you take them out for exercise."

"You mean, babysit them," Annie replied glumly.

"If you want to keep them, yes," he replied briskly. "Now, show me where you're keeping them, and their feed, and I'll give you some pointers on how to keep them healthy."

CHAPTER THREE

Annie led Daniel into the barn, and he took a quick but thorough inventory of the does' bedding, their water, their feed, the air circulation in the barn, and the heat.

To Annie's relief, he declared himself satisfied.

"You're doing most everything right," he told her approvingly. "Just remember to change their bedding out every day – it has to be dry – and whatever you do, don't feed them a lot of grain. It needs to be a good hay mix."

"How do they look to you?" Annie asked.

"Healthy," Daniel told her. "They might be a little mischievous, but they seem strong for their age. You should be able to sell them for a good price this fall, if you keep them as healthy as they are now."

"If I keep them alive, you mean," Annie grumbled.

"Always assuming that you keep them alive," Daniel agreed

dryly.

Annie fell silent for a long moment, squinting down at the does. Then she turned to Daniel and blurted: "If I'm doing everything right with these goats, then why do they hate me?"

Daniel rolled his eyes. "They don't hate you, Annie."

"They're little angels with everyone else," Annie complained, frowning, "like with you right now. But as soon as it's just them and me, they turn into little monsters! It was the same with the buck. He'd love on everybody else, and butt me."

Daniel crossed his arms. "I don't know, Annie. Goats have a bad reputation, but they usually aren't all that mean. Maybe they sense that you're nervous, or that you don't like taking care of them. Animals pick up on that, sometimes."

"Well, I *don't* like taking care of them," Annie mumbled. "They're a pain, and I wish I was rid of them!"

Daniel nodded. "Well, there you go. My advice would be to try to think about something besides how much you don't like them. At least when you're with them."

"Fat chance of that."

They walked outside, and Annie closed the barn up tight behind them. As they walked back to the house, Tim's distant voice made them pause.

"Hey, wait up!"

Tim emerged from the trees at the far edge of the pasture, a good 500 yards away. He clambered over the pasture fence and slogged through the snow to meet them. He was grasping something in his hand, and when he got close, Annie could see that it was a handful of white feathers.

She shaded her eyes against the glare of the snow. "No luck?"

"This is all I could find," her young brother replied, holding them up. "I don't think any of the hens we lost are coming back."

"How many coyotes were there?" Daniel frowned.

"I saw six sets of tracks," Tim told him.

Annie set her mouth glumly. Great. Six, at least, that would remember where they got a good chicken dinner, and where they might still get some goat. She looked up at her brother.

"Well, don't just stand there, holding the feathers," she told him dryly. "They won't do us any good!"

Tim tossed the chicken feathers into the air, they both laughed as Daniel dodged them, crying, "For heaven's sake – get those feathers away!"

Tim looked at him mischievously. "Daniel can't have white feathers sticking to his coat," he laughed. "Then he wouldn't look slicked up for the girls."

Daniel waved them away, but if he was expecting an

apology, he was disappointed. Both of the Miller children laughed wickedly to see him blush.

"Oh, I'm going inside to talk to your father," Daniel muttered, stepping gingerly across the slushy ground. "At least Mose is an adult."

As he disappeared into the house, Tim jabbed Annie in the ribs. "Eh, he's really got it bad! But maybe we shouldn't tease him."

"Maybe not. But sometimes I can't help myself," she retorted. "Daniel's the goober of the world these days. Did you see how shiny his coat was? I bet he brushed it a hundred times. He must be expecting to see Emma today." She shook with silent laughter, and wiped her eyes. "Sometimes I wish he'd just go ahead and marry her, so he could get his brain back."

But Tim wasn't listening to her. He pointed out across the yard to the front of the house, where a shiny gray buggy was just pulling up. "Goober of the world? No, not Daniel," he answered, grinning. "No, that would be Samuel Stauffer.

"Whatcha think he wants *here*, Annie?" he teased, and his sister scowled and pushed his face away with one hand.

"To show off, of course," she murmured, but drifted off slowly across the yard and out to the front porch to meet him, nevertheless.

Samuel was dressed up in his *for-gut* suit, like he was going to worship or something, and he'd scrubbed his face shiny.

Annie shook her head. Tim had been right. Samuel was going to give old Daniel a run for his money when it came to *uber-gooberness*. She wondered who he was after this time, but didn't care enough to wonder long.

"Morning, Samuel," she said, in a matter-of-fact voice. His buggy was shining as if it were wet, and Annie wondered idly if he'd waxed it. She wouldn't put it past him.

Samuel tied his horse to their hitching post and lifted a smiling face to hers. "Morning, Annie! I was in the neighborhood and thought I'd drop by and say hello. Nice morning, isn't it?"

"Oh, sure, yes it is," Annie nodded absently. Her eyes wandered to the black saddlebred. The parts of its coat that weren't covered by its blanket glistened like coal in the wintery sunlight, and its breath made rolling clouds of steam. Samuel's horse really was a glorious specimen, she had to admit it. She sidled closer and ran a hand over its gleaming flank. It was smooth as silk to the touch.

"Had any breakfast?" she asked idly, still looking at the horse.

"Oh, I had a big one back home," Samuel replied stoutly, and Annie nodded. She'd been raised to always offer food to visitors, but she never got any takers, and she didn't expect to get any. Everybody in the county knew that she ruined food and that Tim let the collie eat off the kitchen table.

"I'm going into town to get lunch," Samuel added nonchalantly. "Care to take a spin?"

Annie brushed her hand along the black's silky mane. It might be fun to see the horse go through his paces and see if Samuel had the sense to keep him from running away when a truck passed by.

She looked up, remembering that Samuel had said something. "Say again?"

Samuel tilted his head and frowned. "I said, do you wanna take a spin in the buggy?"

Her eyes returned to the glorious black stallion. "Em – okay," Annie shrugged, and Samuel's face brightened. He held out his hand and Annie took it just long enough to jump up lightly into the buggy.

She settled into the seat, and when she looked up at the house, she just caught sight of a window curtain as it fell back into place and Tim's laughing face. Annie felt her own face going red. She adjusted her cape, and promised herself that she'd put Tim into a head lock if he gave her any grief when she got back. He knew better, anyway. Only a fool would think that she cared a rap for Samuel Stauffer – at least, cared for him out of the ordinary way, as she was supposed to care for everybody.

But she'd said some pretty mean things to Samuel earlier – things about his intelligence and his taste, and about this buggy specifically.

So she decided to extend the olive branch to Samuel Stauffer, in the spirit of tolerance. She figured to make a large gesture, a sacrifice, and resigned herself to suffer the social consequences – as long as they weren't *too* costly.

Samuel climbed up into the seat beside her and shook the reins. But as the buggy rolled away, Annie saw her father's face appear in the window.

His bushy eyebrows were up, his mouth was hanging slightly open and his expression told Annie that he hadn't believed Tim's word.

He had come to see it for himself.

CHAPTER FOUR

It was a fine, cold day with a clear blue sky and a sparkling blanket of snow covered the countryside. The trees were iced like cake, the hills were rounded to gentle, flowing lines, and even the ruts in the road were filled in. The entire landscape was smooth and quiet and blindingly white, and Samuel opened a drawer in the dash and popped on a pair of sunglasses with metallic blue lenses, and a bright orange watch with an LED display that flashed like an electronic road sign.

Annie shook her head and turned her attention to the only other creature nearby that had sense.

The horse.

She watched the black as he trotted down the snowy road. He had a smooth, light pace, and the white winter sunlight danced off his neck as he moved. When he tossed his head, his silky mane rolled back from his neck like a ragged black flag.

He really was the finest horse she'd ever seen, and it pained

Annie to see him pulling a buggy when he was meant to be a pleasure horse.

She turned to Samuel. "Why don't you get another horse to pull your buggy, Samuel? You're wasting this one. He's a pleasure horse, a jumper."

Samuel seemed taken aback by her question. "Another horse? Do you know of a better one? He's the best-looking buggy horse in the county."

Annie shook her head. "Yes, but any horse can pull a buggy. This one's…well, he's too beautiful to be used up on the road. He's a show horse."

Samuel shot her a knowing look. "You want to ride him again, don't you?" he nodded.

"Oh, for—"

"Yes, you do!" Samuel grinned, "I can tell when you get that look in your eye, Annie Miller!"

Annie gazed at the black as it danced over the road. "I just don't want to see a fine, beautiful animal go to waste, that's all," she replied softly.

"Oh, don't worry, Annie," Samuel told her easily. "This is my *rumspringa* horse. He's not for everyday. And I won't have him for long. I'll sell him to some rich Englisher who'll only ride him on Sundays. But, for now, isn't he a fine one?"

The stallion snorted, and white clouds rolled from its

nostrils. Annie tilted her head and gazed at him wistfully.

"Yes, he is," she murmured.

Samuel nodded. "I'll let you ride him again, Annie," he promised gallantly and winked at her. "If you ask me nicely."

"Oh, go boil your head, Samuel Stauffer," she replied, in mild disgust, and Samuel threw his head back and laughed.

Samuel drove into town in a leisurely way, rolling along the back roads when they could've made better time by taking the highway. But Annie decided that it was all right with her that they took the scenic route. For one thing, it was a bright, crisp winter's day, and a beautiful day for a drive. And for another, she didn't necessarily want to advertise to everyone in the county that she was humoring Samuel Stauffer.

People might get the wrong idea.

And sure enough, when they got close to town and began to pass other buggies and pedestrians on the sidewalks, Annie noticed, to her chagrin, that the kids their own age turned to stare at them as Samuel's buggy passed by.

Some of them smirked.

Annie hunched down in the tiger-striped seat, and her eyes moved to the tacky Hawaiian hula doll gyrating on Samuel's console. She was forced to admit that the smirkers had a point, and was tempted to feel like a fool; but she'd decided to make amends for the rude things she's said to Samuel Stauffer, to extend the olive branch. She had no choice now but to stick to that decision.

But when Samuel reached behind her and pulled a boom box out of the back seat, and turned it up to *blasting*, Annie closed her eyes and had to hold her olive branch tight. Samuel's frantic music was a violation of the *ordnung*, and if there was one thing she didn't need, it was to be the subject of the morning sermon, *again*.

Annie shook her head. The boom box was one more example of just how reckless and socially tone-deaf Samuel was. Cranking loud music in the middle of an Amish town was just as good as leaning out the door of the buggy and screaming, *Look at me*.

And people *were* looking.

A group of Amish girls were standing in front of a shop talking to one another, but at the sound of the blasting music, they looked up. Annie cringed as the buggy rolled slowly past. She knew most of the girls from school, and she knew what it meant when they smiled, cast their eyes down and looked at each other.

Annie caught a sudden movement out of the corner of her right eye and turned just in time to keep her face out of a photo. An English tourist looked at his wife and laughed, "I didn't know they listened to gansta rap!"

Samuel laughed and drummed his fingers on the dash in time to the thumping music. But Annie's worried eyes were watching the horse. The stallion was tossing its head and showing ominous signs of agitation. Its ears were turned back, it was snorting, and Annie didn't like the wild look in its eyes. She leaned over and snapped the music off.

Samuel turned to her. "Hey!"

But Annie nodded toward the horse. "If you don't want that black to fly to the moon, and take us with him, Samuel Stauffer, you'd better keep that racket turned off. Look at him!"

Samuel turned to look at the horse and replied thoughtfully: "Guess you're right, Annie." Then, with a smile: "Maybe I should trade him in for a big black truck with speakers in the bed! *Ba boom ba ba boom ba ba boomedy boom boom!*"

Annie rolled her eyes and only barely restrained an expletive.

They turned a corner and rolled off the main drag, for which Annie was deeply thankful; but now they were travelling the fast food strip, and the lane was thick with cars and buggies. And, in spite of the snow, there were also lots of kids on the sidewalk. Annie sat up suddenly.

"Hey, isn't that Aaron and David?"

They turned their heads, and sure enough, it was their friends. Samuel nodded to the two boys as they rolled by, and Annie gave them a wan smile. Her two friends looked up and gaped at them.

David's pudgy face had been wiped blank by astonishment, but Aaron's had been slapped by it. He turned his head to watch them as they passed, and his expression reminded Annie of her father's: brows up, eyes wide, mouth open.

The sight of Aaron's face made Annie go red from the tips of her toes to the ends of her hair. He was probably thinking that she'd lost her mind, and she was beginning to wonder if he was right. She looked sideways at Samuel's profile. With his black hat and blue sunglasses and bright orange wristwatch, he looked like a character from an Amish reality show.

Amish Gone Goober, maybe.

"I'm thinking about having racing flames painted on the side of my buggy," Samuel told her suddenly, grinning. "What do you think, Annie? Orange and red flames – or blue flames, with a laughing skull?"

Annie shook her head grimly, and Samuel chuckled at her expression. "Oh, come on, Annie, lighten up," he told her.

"You won't be happy until you're standing up in front of the church, confessing to everybody what a goober you are," Annie told him. "I'm just glad I won't be there with you."

Samuel's only answer was to pucker his lips and blow her an air kiss, and Annie waved him away, muttering.

To Annie's surprise, Samuel drove right past the usual fast food restaurants and made for the Smokin' Hot. The Smokin' Hot was a fancy local sub shop. The owners baked their own bread and then stuffed the loaf with fresh produce, herb mayonnaise, and gourmet meats and cheeses. Most of the kids she knew considered it a special treat, because it was an expensive place to buy lunch. Annie picked up her purse and consulted her wallet.

Samuel saw her do it.

"Hey, now, you don't think I'd ask you to lunch and then make you pay?" he objected, with a comical face. "It's my treat today, Annie."

"No it isn't," Annie replied. She had satisfied herself that she had enough mad money to cover the insane price they asked for a sandwich and a drink.

"Oh, come on, now Annie," Samuel teased her. "Aren't you always the one lecturing me about *hochmut*?"

Annie went red to the ears, but shook her head. "I have money of my own, Samuel Stauffer. I'll buy my own lunch."

"Suit yourself then, Annie Miller," he laughed, and shook the reins.

The Smokin' Hot was a plain, white, two story building that looked like a house. It had a small wooden sign over the door, and that was all. The restaurant was well off the beaten track, and on a cold, snowy day, the locals had it pretty much to themselves.

Samuel stopped the buggy and jumped out to tie up to a hitching post. Then he walked carefully around to Annie's side and opened the door for her, like a gentleman. Annie raised her eyebrow.

"You needn't to grin at me like a big goober, Samuel Stauffer," she told him tartly. "I can get out of this buggy by myself."

Samuel looked down at the icy lot and tilted his head. "Can you skate?" he asked innocently.

"Better than you, and you know it," Annie retorted defiantly, and jumped down. But to her chagrin, her foot landed sideways on the ice and went out from under her. She grabbed for the buggy, but what she caught was Samuel.

He grabbed her arm and pulled her into his chest, with her face smushed right up against his coat.

"*Lfme guh,*" she mumbled, and slipped again.

Samuel laughed and put his arms around her shoulders. "Not so fast, Annie! So you skate better than me? My, my."

"*Shudp.*"

"Put your arm around my waist, and I'll hold your shoulder like so, and maybe we'll make it across the parking lot."

"I can do it myself."

"No you can't."

Annie pushed away from him, almost fell, and landed up on his chest again. Samuel grabbed her arm and pulled her to his side, and together they did an unintentional dance across the ice.

Annie set her mouth grimly and did her best to stay upright. She was keenly aware that they both looked like fools, and that anyone driving by was getting a show at their expense. Samuel suddenly slid, yelled, and flailed, and they both almost fell down; but he caught himself at the last minute, caught her when she threatened to go down with him, struggled up, and yanked her along with him over the ice, and to the safety of the restaurant.

They grabbed the handrails beside the entryway steps and bent over them weakly. Then Samuel cackled crazily and jabbed her in the ribs.

Annie glanced over at his laughing blue eyes and cracked up in spite of herself. But she added: "You're nuts, Samuel. Next time I'm staying home."

When they opened the door and walked in, the waitress at the counter smiled at them.

"We were watching you two from the window," she told them. "We didn't think you'd make it! You're good on ice, kid," she told Samuel, with a wink. "You must play hockey."

Annie looked up at Samuel wryly. He could live for a year

on praise, and sure enough, he looked three inches taller. He rolled his eyes to hers and grinned, and Annie gave him a dry look.

The waitress pulled out an order pad. "What'll you have?"

Samuel looked at her, and Annie replied: "I'll have the bread bowl."

"What kind of soup?"

"French Onion."

"And you, hockey boy?"

Samuel went a little red around the ears, but looked pleased. "I'll have the monster."

"Regular or premium meat?"

"Premium."

"Alone or combo?"

"Combo."

"One check?"

Annie looked up at her sharply. "Two." She handed over her money, and Samuel took his hat off and handed over most of a clipped wad of cash.

"Coming up."

The dining room was mostly empty on such a cold day, but

there were a few other people seated in odd corners, mostly English locals minding their own business. Samuel led Annie to a corner booth away from the others and they settled in.

Annie gave him a direct look. "Why on earth did you want to come out on such a snowy day, just to have this fancy lunch?" she challenged him. "It's like burning your money in the fireplace!"

Samuel raised his brows and grinned. "Why? Because it's fun to get out," he told her, shaking out his napkin, "and because I wanted to drive the black, and because the monster was calling my name."

Annie shook her head. "You should be saving your money," she told him. "You're gonna need it for rent when you move out of your parent's house."

"Oh, I don't worry about that, Annie," he told her, more soberly. "I'll always be working, so there'll always be money. And anyway, what good is money if you don't enjoy it?"

"Well, it's your life," Annie shrugged, "but if I were you, I'd be saving like a squirrel."

Samuel grinned at her and held up the slender clip of bills. "You see this, Annie? It's all the money I've got in the world."

Annie felt her mouth falling open. She gaped at him in disbelief.

"What?"

"That's right. I have"—he unfolded it—"Three dollars and sixty-two cents."

"You mean you just spent the last of your money on a sub combo?"

He waved away her objection, smiling. "Don't fret about it, Annie! I never do. It always works out in the end. Remember," he added piously, "worry is a sin."

Annie stared at him incredulously, and clamped her mouth shut for fear of what might come out of it. She was spared further temptation when the waitress called, "Your order's ready!"

Samuel got up to go get it, and Annie was left to stare after him in amazement.

She shook her head. Samuel Stauffer didn't have the sense that God gave a chicken. Why, he'd even offered to pay for her lunch!

And when Samuel came back with their food, Annie found that his confession had quite taken her appetite away. She picked at her meal, because she was helping her foolish friend devour the last penny he had on earth.

But Samuel smiled at her, sat down to his huge meal with gusto, and appeared – to Annie's annoyance – to enjoy every last crumb of it.

CHAPTER FIVE

When they were back in Samuel's buggy again, Samuel popped his shiny blue sunglasses back on his face and turned to ask:

"Whadya wanna do now?"

Annie looked at him grimly. "You'd better go back home and do some work, Samuel Stauffer. You're broke."

Samuel shook his head. "Always looking on the dark side, Annie! You should lighten up…seriously."

Annie opened her mouth to deliver her soul, but then remembered that she'd been way too direct with Samuel already, and this outing was supposed to be about her extending the olive branch. So she closed her eyes and swallowed what she'd been about to say. Samuel looked down at her in amusement.

His expression told her that he'd read that thought right off her face, and that it cracked him up. Annie crossed her arms and hunched down in the seat, thinking of all the things that she *could* say about Samuel Stauffer's big empty head, and the need for him to get some common sense to bounce around in it and, hopefully, hit the side somewhere.

That is, if only she wasn't restrained by tolerance, and the spirit of Christian meekness.

But by the time they had cleared town, and were rolling along the pretty, snowy little dirt lane roads, Annie mellowed again. It was too pretty a day to be angry, and the pleasant drive made her forget her disgust with Samuel's foolishness. It was a sparkling day, not too cold – nearly perfect. And after his rest at the Smokin' Hot, the black seemed ready for a run. He tossed his head and snorted and pulled at the reins now and then.

Samuel laughed and shook them. "Look at him fret! I think he wants to run, don't you, Annie?"

Annie glanced up at Samuel and smiled just a bit, because he had stumbled across her secret wish.

"Watch this, Annie," Samuel grinned and shook the reins hard. The black quickened his pace, and they went rolling down the road at a sharp clip. Samuel put the buggy smack in the middle of the road, and drove over the center like a fearless man.

Annie laughed in spite of herself. She loved going fast, and Samuel knew it.

"I'd like to see that black of yours really cut loose. I bet he's the fastest horse in the county," she replied wistfully.

Samuel lifted his chin. "I *know* he is," he grinned and pointed to the rearview. Annie looked into it, and saw another buggy in the distance, coming up fast behind them.

Samuel turned the black's head and moved the buggy over to the snowy shoulder. The other buggy soon came rolling up alongside, and the Amish boy driving it leaned over to say:

"Well, well, Samuel Stauffer! Out with the black again, I see! How'd you like to race him against my gray?"

Samuel looked at the boy's buggy horse – a lean, fiery gray, gnashing at the bit.

"My black'll make your gray eat dirty snow," Samuel laughed.

"Oh, he will? Put your money where your mouth is." The boy raised a thick wad of bills in his hand and waved it in the air. "Two hundred dollars says that my gray reaches the Big Oak turnoff first."

Annie's eyes bugged out and she shot Samuel an urgent look, but he wasn't even turned her way.

"Done. We'll start on three. One..."

Annie leaned over and hissed: "Samuel!"

"Two..."

"Are you crazy?"

"Three!"

Samuel shouted and shook the reins; the black scrambled forward, and they went flying down the narrow, snowy road. Samuel leaned over and yanked the reins sharply, and their buggy lurched wildly to the left and pushed the other buggy right off the road. The other boy had to drive right over the shoulder to avoid a crash, and Samuel laughed.

""Hey, get up!" he shouted, and the black flattened its ears and quickened its pace. The other boy was shouting to his horse, too, and he pushed back into the road, forcing Samuel to bounce off on the rough right shoulder.

Annie grabbed the bobbing dash and watched as a split rail fence zoomed up on the right, inches from her window.

"Samuel!" she cried.

Samuel shook the reins. "Come on!"

The black surged past the gray, but the gray replied, flashing past them like a blue blur, and they were pushed out of the road again, and went bouncing over the snow-covered grass. They were speeding toward the top of a hill, and Annie's heart jumped in her chest, because when she looked ahead, she saw that the road narrowed dramatically between two big trees.

There *was* no right-hand shoulder any more.

"*Samuel!*" she screamed.

Samuel shook the reins and yelled urgently, and the black flattened its ears and throttled down for an extra gear.

Annie watched in a mixture of horror and excitement as the black surged ahead, then pushed its way into the road, forcing the other buggy over and then sharply back, as the boy yanked hard on the reins and fell behind them. They flashed through the archway of the trees and roared down the long, flat stretch to the Big Oak turnoff, a fork in the road 500 yards ahead.

The trees fell away and the shoulders were suddenly open again. Annie looked back and saw the other boy slapping the reins against the gray's back, heard him shouting encouragement. The gray began to gain on them.

"Come on, Samuel!" Annie shouted, and Samuel leaned forward in his seat to give the black his head. Annie watched the black in fascination. It was running like a racehorse now. Its hooves were pounding a wild drumbeat, its ears were laid flat, and its glorious mane thrashed in the air like a battle flag as it tossed its head and neighed wildly.

Out of the corner of her eye, Annie caught sight of the gray's straining neck creeping up past the back wheel of their buggy, and the other driver's open mouth, yelling. Her eyes drifted over Samuel's clenched jaw and taut fists. Then he turned to look at her through his shiny blue sunglasses, and cracked a grin from ear to ear.

The Big Oak turnoff flashed past, and Samuel tossed the reins into the air, and the black eased off as they bounced to a long, smooth stop on the deserted road. Annie leaned back into the seat and closed her eyes. Her own heartbeat, and Samuel's delighted laughter, was thrumming in her ears.

The other buggy rattled up behind, and Samuel leaned across her to shout: "What did I tell you?"

"You got lucky," the other boy gibed, but tossed the wad of cash into the buggy. Samuel caught it in his hand and gave his rival a jaunty salute.

"I'll see you again next month," the boy called, and Samuel laughed.

"We'll be here!"

The buggy rolled off, and Samuel tossed the wad of cash up into the air and caught it with one hand. Annie rolled her eyes to Samuel's, and he winked at her.

"What did I tell you, Annie?" he demanded triumphantly. "It always works out!"

Annie cracked a reluctant grin. She should tell him, of course, that he was a fool, that gambling was against the *ordnung*, that racing was against it too, and that if he thought the universe was going to send money flowing into his lap, he was crazy.

But instead, she cracked up and laughed like a crazy thing. And she suddenly remembered why she always put up with Samuel's bragging and foolishness.

Samuel Stauffer might be full of bluster and nonsense, but he was always doing something fun, even if he had to spend his very last dime, and he never felt the least bit guilty about it.

And when she was with him, she had fun, too.

Samuel laughed with her, and on an impulse, he leaned over and gave her a peck on the forehead.

And later that evening, when Annie opened her bag and took out her wallet, she discovered that she had about 15 dollars more than she should have.

About what her lunch had cost.

Annie put a hand on her hip, and shook her head, and blessed Samuel Staffer out under her breath. She'd have to give it back, of course.

But she couldn't keep herself from laughing just a little, too, all the same.

CHAPTER SIX

Isaac Muller walked through the fresh morning snow to his woodworking shop, just to the side of his barn. To his surprise, the shop door was standing slightly ajar, and he frowned as he opened it and walked in.

Everything was just where he had left it: his worktable was neat and tidy, and his woodworking tools were placed neatly to one side.

But something was different. *Very* different.

Isaac wrinkled his nose. A pungent odor filled the shop. It was indescribably bad, and it seemed to be coming from somewhere around his worktable.

He bent down and peered underneath. A small puddle stained the floor, and a small, dark stain branched off of it, up one leg of the workbench and across the top. And not *just* across the top.

Across every piece of the chisel set that he had left lying on the table.

Isaac picked up one of his chisels. He turned it over in his hand and then lifted it gingerly to his nose.

He closed his eyes, made a terrible face, and set it quickly back down.

A sound from the doorway made him turn his head. There in the opening stood the triumphant buck. It pawed the floor and glared at him with its beady yellow eyes, and stamped.

Isaac's placid brow gathered thunder. "Why you little—"

The goat bleated at him and ran away, and Isaac was left to scoop his chisels into a bowl and carry them off, muttering, to the sink in the bathroom.

A little later on, toward noon, when it was as bright and warm as it would be all day, his wife Cora led their toddler, Isaac Joseph, out into the front yard to enjoy the sunshine and to play in the snow.

Cora shaded her eyes and looked up at the top of their house. The buck had climbed up on the roof again, and was staring down at them from his kingly perch just below their bedroom window.

Isaac Joseph shrieked with laughter. He beat the snowy ground with his feet in excitement.

Cora knelt down beside him and pointed up to the roof. "That's right, it's funny!" she laughed. "What is that, Isaac Joseph? Tell Mamm what it is!"

"Goat!" he cried, "Goat, goat!"

"That's right, it's the goat," Cora laughed, and kissed his cheek. "Isn't he naughty, to climb up on our roof?"

Isaac emerged just then from his workshop and walked back toward the house. Cora called to him and turned to Isaac Joseph. "See, there's Daed," she told him. "Let's wave to him! Wave!"

Isaac Joseph stuck his hands up in the air and waved wildly. His father looked up and saw them, and his face brightened. He smiled and waved with one big hand.

But the buck turned a wrathful yellow eye on the presuming male that had intruded on its royal domain. It lowered his head, and stamped its foot smartly on the roof – once, twice, three times.

And the foot of snow that had packed up on the sloping roof cracked, broke, and came pouring off like a white waterfall – right on Isaac's head.

"Oh, Isaac!"

Isaac was knocked off his feet, and a cloud roiled up into the air. When it cleared, Isaac was sitting in a pile of snow up to his neck, and his face was as white as an iced cookie.

Cora gasped, fought the impulse to burst out laughing, and called in a quavering voice: "Isaac, are you…are you all right?"

Isaac shook the snow out of his hair and slowly rose from the white mound, dusting his clothes. "Yes." He looked up at the goat grimly. The buck held his eye, snorted, and stamped again. The remnants of snow left on the roof poured down in little white rivulets.

Cora turned to the baby. "Doesn't Daed look funny?" she whispered, and Isaac Joseph clapped his hands and laughed.

Isaac came striding across the yard, and held out his hand for his son. Isaac Joseph went running to take it, and Isaac knelt down and spoke quietly into his ear.

"Let's make a snowman, buddy. I'll come back in a minute and build him up. Can you find a couple of sticks for his arms? And a few little rocks? We'll make a face for him."

Isaac Joseph laughed and turned to hunt for some sticks, and Isaac stood up and walked over to Cora.

Cora reached up to pick ice crystals out of her husband's hair, and suppressed the laughter that bubbled up in her throat.

He stared down at her. "Cora, that goat has got to go."

Cora looked up at him, and her expression changed. Her blue eyes were full of sudden dismay. "Oh no, Isaac, not the little goat! The baby loves it!"

"The baby loves everything. We'll get him another pet."

"Oh, Isaac, no!"

"It's *mean*, Cora."

"Oh, now, just because it dumped some snow on your head! It was an accident!"

"It pees on everything. I went into the shop this morning. It had peed on my tools, Cora."

Cora tried desperately not to laugh, failed, and Isaac's face went red.

"You can laugh if you want, Cora, but I mean it. The goat has got to go."

Cora dimpled. "I'm sorry, Isaac, but you look so funny. Your face is all in a knot. And you've even got snow on your eyelashes!"

Isaac rubbed his eyes with a big knuckle, but refused to laugh.

"Daed, look!" Isaac Joseph called, and held out two crooked sticks in one chubby hand, and a fistful of rocks in the other.

"That's good! Let's put them on."

He turned back to Cora, and his expression softened. "I'm sorry, Cora. I know you and Isaac Joseph like the goat. But I'm going to put him up for sale."

Cora's lip pushed out slightly, and Isaac shook his head. "It's no use to give me that look, Cora," he warned. "The goat has to go."

Cora looked up mournfully at the roof, but the buck wasn't there anymore. It had sensed that the action was now on the ground, and had jumped down onto the woodpile, and then to the yard.

It arrived just in time to see Isaac Joseph's little bottom sticking out as he bent down to pick up a twig.

Isaac Joseph held it up for his father to see. "This one, Daed!"

Isaac smiled and turned back, and just in time. The buck snorted, reared up on its hind legs and went charging toward its target.

"Isaac, the baby!" Cora shrieked, and his father grabbed Isaac Joseph safely up into the air seconds before the goat came zooming past.

Cora's mouth formed a horrified O, and the look on her face was that of sudden, blinding revelation.

"Oh, the hateful thing!"

She rushed over, scooped the baby into her arms, and hurried back inside to the safety of the house – abandoning the buck to the wrath of her husband.

Isaac looked at the goat grimly. It circled around to face him, and stood stiff-legged in the snow, staring him down defiantly. Then it opened its mouth and bleated a challenge.

Isaac marched over, grabbed it unceremoniously by its horns, twisted its head, and dragged it back to the pen. The goat snorted and kicked, but it was no match for Isaac Muller's muscular arms.

Isaac pushed the buck into the pen and locked the door fast behind it. The buck turned, and they stared at one another through the wire fence.

"Soon," Isaac promised, and the buck hiked its leg and shot a stream of pee toward the door. Isaac dodged away with a shocked exclamation, and threw a snowball at the animal's head before retiring to the house in disgust.

CHAPTER SEVEN

That evening found the bishop, Joseph Lapp, relaxing in the bosom of his family. It was about an hour after dinner, and his wife and youngest daughter were with him in the living room. He settled comfortably in his big stuffed chair, folded his copy of *Die Botschaft* together and turned the page. After awhile he turned and addressed his wife, Katie, who was sitting opposite him on the couch, brushing their little daughter's hair.

"*Huh.* It looks like Isaac is selling that goat he bought from us," Joseph told her, and gave her a straight look from over the top of the paper.

Katie raised her brows innocently. "Oh?"

"Yes. He's running an ad in the paper. He's practically giving it away. I wonder why." He turned the page.

"I do, too," Katie replied. "The baby loved it, and Cora seemed taken with it, too."

"Cora's taken with everything," he replied dryly, and Katie pursed her lips and gave him a admonishing look.

"You know, Katie, maybe it would be a good idea for us to rethink our goat, as well," he added, and their little daughter looked up in dismay.

"Oh no, Daed," she wailed, "not little Martha! That's *my* goat, and when she's old enough, she'll give us milk and cheese!" She fixed pleading blue eyes on her father's face.

Katie gave her husband another speaking look, and he shook out his newspaper and cleared his throat.

"It was just a thought."

He turned the page again, read in silence for few moments, and then frowned. "Those coyotes are really becoming a menace. Abel Zook reports that he lost fifteen chickens last month."

"That's terrible!"

"I heard Mose Miller say that coyotes hit their farm, too, the other night. He only lost a handful of chickens, though. He told me that Annie rushed out and shot two of the coyotes and the others ran away."

Katie looked up in surprise. "Annie shot them?"

Her husband didn't look up. "*Mmm.* Mose tells me that Annie's a good shot. Sometimes she even goes hunting with him."

"Mose shouldn't encourage her," Katie mumbled, and pulled her daughter's hair tight.

"I don't know," Joseph replied, turning the page. "Those coyotes are getting out of control. We're going to have to get another hunting party together, and another rifle hand might come in handy."

"Oh, Joseph, for heaven's sake."

Her husband's lips curled up a little, but he forbore to tease her further.

Katie frowned and plaited her daughter's shining brown hair with skillful fingers. Presently, she ventured:

"You know, Joseph, it's been a while since we visited Mose and his children. Maybe we should go over there one afternoon."

Joseph nodded. "It's all right with me."

"Ow, Mamm!" Dorathea yelped, and Katie looked down. She had pulled the hair band too tight, and snapped her little daughter's ear by mistake.

"Oh, I'm sorry, baby," she cried, and rubbed the pink spot with her fingers. "I wasn't keeping my mind on what I was doing." She bit her lip, and secured Dorathea's braid again.

"I know what you're thinking," her husband told her quietly. "But you're going to have to settle down to it, Katie. Annie is never going to be giggly or girly like Cora. If that's what you're trying to make her, you're just going to end up frustrated."

Katie shot him a look that was almost fiery by her mild standards, and Joseph raised his brows. "We both know it's true," he added quietly.

"What I know, Joseph Lapp, is that my poor niece is so far behind the other girls her age that she needs all the help she can get. Not a lot of discouraging talk." She patted her daughter's hair, and kissed her ear, and Dorathea rose and skipped up the stairs.

"But now that you mention Cora, she might be able to help," Katie nodded. "If anyone can make Annie see the importance of-of dressing neat and looking her best, it would be Cora. Cora loves to look as nice as she can, and maybe some of that will rub off on Annie, if she's with her."

"Cora's a married woman and a mother. She should have a more serious mind than that, by now."

Katie burst out laughing and put her hand over her mouth. "You know better," she giggled. "Last Sunday I saw her pull a tube of lip gloss out of her bag. And don't you scold her about it, Joseph Lapp! Poor Cora – she loves it so!"

Joseph lowered the paper and frowned. "Really? Lip gloss?"

"Mostly clear."

"That's against the *ordnung*," Joseph mumbled, and went back to his paper.

"I'm thankful every day that she lives in a church district where her brother is the bishop," Katie told him. "If she were even two districts over, poor Cora would be miserable. And so would a lot of others," she added, looking more serious.

Joseph lowered his paper. "What do you mean? Am I supposed to be the easy bishop?"

Katie smiled at him affectionately. "Let's say, the kind, wise bishop," she amended, "who knows that it's sometimes more important to have compassion, than to be strict on every little point."

"The easy bishop," Joseph nodded, as if his fears had been confirmed. Katie smiled, and came over and pushed in between her husband and his paper. She settled down on his lap and put her arms around his neck.

Joseph embraced her and looked into her eyes. "Don't be so sure of me," he told her gravely. "Next Sunday, I will shock you all. I'll preach a sermon that will have everyone hiding under the benches!"

His pretty wife didn't look alarmed. She rubbed his nose with a small finger. "Oh?"

Joseph sat up a little straighter, and tightened his hold on her. His blue eyes kindled with inspiration. "That's right, a sermon that will strike every heart like a thunderbolt!"

"My, my!"

"I will preach on the dangers of eating too much sausage, and fried potatoes, and cake! I will smite the pie-eating sinners that are getting fat!" he cried, and buried his face into his giggling wife's neck.

But after Katie had a chance to settle down, a more thoughtful look replaced her smiles. She turned to Joseph with a serious look.

"You're not saying that you think I'm getting fat – are you, Joseph Lapp?"

Her husband's startled blue eyes looked up at hers, and his mouth fell open in dismay. But he was a wise enough man to know that there was no good way out of the trap he'd stumbled into, and so he ended the conversation with an abrupt kiss.

And to his relief – his wife was also a minister of mercy.

CHAPTER EIGHT

The sound of horse's hooves approaching on the road outside caused Tim Miller to stop reading his copy of *Captain Space,* and to close it quickly inside the pages of the *Young Companion.* He got up from the couch and pulled the curtains aside.

Then he turned to his father with a look of wide-eyed panic on his freckled face. "It's the bishop!"

Mose looked up sharply, snapped his copy of *The Budget* shut and stuffed it under the cushion of his chair. "Annie!" he called, "It's your aunt and uncle! Take those dirty dishes off of the table! Tim, get your collie out of here!"

Annie hurried to the kitchen and grabbed an armful of dishes and dumped them unceremoniously into the sink. She plugged the sink, ran hot water, and squirted dish soap into the water, so the foaming bubbles would at least hide the remnants of their breakfast. She only had time to wet a dish towel, and swipe the crumbs off the table, before the sound of heavy footsteps, and a brisk knock, announced that her uncle and aunt were at the door.

Mose stood up and brushed the front of his sweater before walking to the door. He reached over and opened it.

"Why, it's Joseph and Katie! Come in, come in! What a surprise!"

Joseph ducked his head to clear the top of the door and walked in, followed by Katie.

"We haven't been over to visit in such a long time," Katie smiled. "We were missing all of you."

"Please sit down!" Mose told them, gesturing toward the couch. "Annie, put a little coffee on, and make some sandwiches. Tim, bring another chair."

"Oh, we've already eaten," Katie assured him, "but hot coffee would be nice, after the drive. It's still a bit chilly."

Joseph sat down on the sofa opposite Mose' chair, and the two men settled in to chat as Tim sunk down into a chair and tried his best to look invisible.

Annie went to put the pot on, and rummaged in the refrigerator for cream. To her surprise, she looked up to see Katie at her elbow.

"I'll help you," she volunteered, and Annie went red to the ears.

"Um...that's nice of you, Aunt Katie, but..."

Katie opened the refrigerator door wider, and paused momentarily. The inside of the box was crammed with half empty jars, shriveled fruit, store bought meat of indeterminate age, and several moldy cheeses.

"Ah...sorry about the mess," Annie apologized, in deep embarrassment. "I haven't cleaned it out in awhile."

Katie inhaled, and straightened. "Well," she said briskly, "why don't we do it now?"

Annie goggled at her. "But...you're a guest!"

"No, I'm your aunt," Katie corrected, "and that means I get to help you as often as I like. Where's an apron?"

Annie reluctantly fetched one from a drawer, and Katie tied it around herself. "Cleaning the fridge doesn't take long," she said bracingly, seeing Annie's dubious face. "It's just sorting, really. Let's take everything out, clean and sort, and then replace the things we need."

Annie cringed, and wished herself away, but with her aunt standing right in front of her, there was nothing for it but to start unpacking the refrigerator.

It was harder work than she thought. A jar of maraschino cherries had spilled, and the ancient syrup had cemented itself so firmly to the bottom of the fridge, that it had to be chiseled free with a blunt knife. A container of ancient apples had freeze dried and were covered in strange white spots; and there was a mossy green *something* in the very back that Annie couldn't even identify.

But Annie had to admire her aunt's efficiency. Katie helped her empty the entire contents of the refrigerator in less than 15 minutes, and once it was empty, they set to scrubbing it clean. Annie removed the shelves and took them to the sink, where she washed them, scrubbed them with a scouring pad, and dried them.

Katie had pulled a chair over to the front of the fridge, and was sitting in it. She was obliged to brace her feet against the floor to get the leverage she needed to scrape the grunge off the bottom of the stained shelves, and Annie felt a full-body wave of shame crawl up from her feet to the roots of her hair.

Katie had breathed not a word of rebuke, but Annie was so embarrassed that she vowed to herself that no one was ever going to come in and find her kitchen in such a state ever again.

The kitchen was a pain, and cooking was a bore, but nothing could be more humiliating that having another woman come into your kitchen and have to clean it out.

Even if that other woman was your aunt.

Annie supplied Katie with fresh scouring pads, and in about 15 more minutes, she had scrubbed the refrigerator shiny. When she was finished, Annie stared at it open-mouthed. It hadn't looked that good since they'd bought it – three years earlier.

Katie pushed a tendril of hair back from her brow and sighed. "Whew! That's over. Now we can start putting your things back in."

Annie handed her jars and bottles and jugs, and Katie wiped them clean with a dish rag and placed them in neat rows on the shelves. When she was finished, she stood up and surveyed her work.

"What do you think?" she smiled.

Annie stared at the box in amazement. "I never would've believed that it could look so good," she confessed.

"Now," Katie added, drying her hands, "wipe the fridge door down, and I'll start on the counters."

Annie obeyed, and when she finished she turned to see Katie standing in front of the sink, washing the dishes she'd tried so hard to hide. She had already scrubbed the countertops shiny, and even the pots and pans were arranged neatly on one side.

Annie tilted her head slightly to one side and stared at her aunt in wistful fascination as Katie burned through the dishes. Her imagination slowly blurred Katie's features and painted in those of her smiling mother.

See Annie, her mother was saying, *It's a skill. The Fisher women are all expert housekeepers. I was, and Katie is. See how tidy and pleasant everything looks!*

But even when Annie shook her head and came back to herself, she still saw her aunt through a haze of admiration. Her Aunt Katie was more than kind – she was strong and organized and fast. She had whipped that disaster of a kitchen into shape in less than 30 minutes, and then made it sound as if it was no big deal.

But Annie knew, better than anyone else, that it *was* a big deal.

Katie was a ninja, like out of one of Tim's comic books. And Annie decided that it might not be such a bad thing to be strong and organized and fast like Katie.

And her mother.

She wanted to be a ninja, too – kind of.

And when they took the coffee to the others, Mose looked up toward the kitchen and froze as if he'd seen a ghost. He blinked, shook his head and wiped his eyes.

Annie watched him in awe. "What is it, Daed?"

"What have you two done?" he asked, in a quavering voice. "Your mother's kitchen hasn't looked that way…in years."

Annie shot Katie a small, grateful look, and Katie reached over and squeezed her hand. "*See, Annie,*" she whispered. "*You can do it!*"

And, looking at her aunt's smiling face, Annie almost believed that she could.

CHAPTER NINE

They settled down into the living room to chat, and Annie sank down into a chair next to Katie's, at the edge of the living room.

Her Uncle Joseph leaned forward on the couch and grasped his knees. He was too big and tall for their couch, and he looked uncomfortable to Annie. His expression was troubled, too. Her uncle had bright blue eyes – too bright for Annie sometimes, who knew them mostly from church – but at the moment, they looked clouded and dark.

Worried.

"That's five farms hit this month," he was saying to her father, "and more coyote sightings than ever. And not just at night – some people have told me that they've seen them by the side of the road in broad daylight!"

"We'll never be able to push them out," Mose answered, shaking his head. "There are too many now. The best we can hope is to cut the numbers down and protect our stock as best we can." He looked over at Katie and added, "My Aunt Mary told me last week that she even saw one of them stalking a toddler – in its own yard!"

Katie gasped aloud and rolled her eyes to Joseph's. He met her gaze with a worried look.

"This winter has been so cold, it's driving them out of the woods and out into our farmland," Mose lamented, lifting a mug of coffee to his lips. "They've learned that it's easier to snatch a chicken or a dog than to hunt."

Joseph tightened his mouth to a straight line. "The county keeps telling us that they're shy, and not dangerous," he rumbled, "and that they aren't a threat. Well, that's not what I'm hearing from the people."

"The ones here are half wolf," Mose told him. "Annie killed two of them the other night, and we could see it. They're bigger than coyotes should be, and bolder."

Joseph nodded. "We'll have to go out hunting again. But you're right, that won't be enough. We have to find better ways to protect our livestock and keep them away from our homes." He turned his eyes to Tim, who was sitting quietly in the corner.

"Tim, how would you like to come with us to hunt coyotes?" he asked.

Mose turned to Tim, smiling. "It would be his first group hunt. I've taken him out a few times with me, but never for anything as big."

Tim looked up and managed a weak smile, but rolled his eyes to his father's.

Annie looked back and forth between them. "I could go with you," she offered. "I have Daed's old rifle, and I go out hunting with him all the time."

Joseph smiled and shook his head. "No, Annie, this would just be for the men and boys. Hunting can be dangerous."

Annie opened her mouth and was about to plead her case, but Katie reached over and put a hand on hers. Annie looked up at her, understood the unspoken comment, and swallowed her argument.

But disappointment stuck in her throat like a big, hard lump, and for the thousandth time, Annie wondered why there were so many things that she couldn't do.

Just because she was a girl.

The conversation moved on to other topics, but Annie zoned out. She sat quietly in her chair with her hands folded in her lap, but she was thinking of the hawk she had once seen flying in a blue winter's sky. She wished that at least once in her life, she could be that free.

She closed her eyes, imagining it – what it would be like to soar on the wind in a sparkling sky, with nothing in her way all the way to the horizon.

Free to go wherever she pleased, and to do whatever she wanted.

She wasn't sure how long she daydreamed of flying in the sky, but the sound of knocking on the front door made her fall abruptly back down to earth.

"Annie, can you go and see who it is?" her father asked, and she rose reluctantly and went to the door.

When she opened it, to her surprise, Aaron Graber was standing there in his black hat and coat. Annie's brows rose. She hadn't been expecting Aaron.

"Hi, Aaron."

"Hi Annie. I see you have company." He gestured toward the buggy in the yard. "I can come back later."

"No, come on in," she told him, opening the door. "It's just my aunt and uncle."

Aaron's eyes widened, but it was too late to retreat gracefully, and he took off his hat and came inside.

"Well, hello Aaron," Mose called genially. "We haven't seen you in awhile. Sit down and visit with us. Would you like some coffee?"

"Oh no, thank you," Aaron said quietly, and sat down near the door.

"We were just talking about a hunting trip we're going to

organize," Joseph told him. "There are too many coyotes around here and they're killing stock. We're going to meet one day this month and hunt them. Would you like to go with us?"

"Yes, I would," Aaron told him. "They got one of my dogs last Saturday. One of my best hunters, too!"

Annie shot him a sympathetic look. Aaron had one of the best pack of hunting dogs in the county, and it was a sad loss.

But she also felt an unseemly twinge of resentment, even though her friend Aaron was a natural choice for such a task. Aaron loved to hunt, and he was a good shot.

But *she* could bring a bird down out of the sky, and everyone in the room knew it.

It wasn't fair.

Aaron's voice brought her back to the present. "Yeah, I saw some tracks by the road the other day. I was walking down the road to the Big Oak turnoff, and there were some coyote prints crossing it."

Annie looked up at him, and her mouth dropped open slightly.

"That wasn't all I saw in the snow," Aaron went on evenly. His eyes flitted to Annie's briefly. "There were racing tracks for miles. Two buggies, driving more off the road than on it."

Annie felt her face going hot, and she stared at her friend in disbelief. Aaron was ratting her out!

She bit her lip and lowered her eyes. She didn't want anyone to read the anger off her face, but she was so shocked and mad that she wasn't sure that she could prevent it.

"One of the buggies almost cracked up on a tree," Aaron continued quietly. "The wheel marks missed it by less than a foot."

Mose shook his head. "Some young fool," was his comment. "Don't we have enough buggy accidents!"

"Whoever it is, word will get back to me sooner or later," Joseph added significantly. "And when it does, someone will have a lot of explaining to do. To me *and* to the church."

Annie ventured to look up. Mose was nodding, Tim was looking at Aaron with an awed expression, and Aaron was staring at the floor.

But they didn't worry her half as much as Katie.

Her aunt was looking at *her*. And her knowing expression told Annie that she suspected immediately what most of the rest of them hadn't yet guessed.

CHAPTER TEN

Katie leaned in and hugged Annie close. "We want you to come over and visit us, Annie," she whispered, as they paused in the doorway to say their goodbyes.

Annie smiled – genuinely – and looked up at her. "I will."

Katie kissed her cheek. "See that you do."

Mose followed them out onto the porch and called after Joseph. "Just let us know which day everyone can go hunting," he was saying.

"I will. I'll announce it next Sunday at worship."

Annie stood beside her father on the porch and waved as her aunt and uncle climbed back into their buggy. Katie waved again from the window, and the buggy rolled off at a brisk clip across the snow.

Mose returned inside, but in spite of the cold, Annie stayed put. She knew that Aaron wasn't far behind, and she was waiting for him.

Sure enough, in a few minutes the door opened again and Aaron appeared in the doorway. "I'll bring my dogs," he was saying. "I'll see you all next Sunday."

But when he closed the door behind him, Annie rounded on him angrily. She crossed her arms and nodded.

"You've got a fine nerve, Aaron Graber," she growled, "to come to my own house to rat me out to my Daed. And to the bishop, too!"

Aaron's cheeks went red, but he held her eye. "I didn't rat you out, Annie. I didn't tell them *who*. But someone has to put a stop to it. Samuel almost killed you both. You missed that tree by inches!"

"You don't have to tell me that," Annie snapped. "I was there! And if I want to go buggy racing with Samuel Stauffer, it's my own business."

"Samuel's crazy and he always has been," Aaron retorted. "But you have better sense than to do that kind of thing, Annie. I'm surprised at you!"

Her sensible friend's rebuke struck a nerve, and Annie felt herself going red. It was true that Samuel was crazy, and she couldn't deny it. But it was her business and her neck.

"Well you can go right on being surprised," Annie told him hotly, "because if I want to go buggy riding with Samuel

Stauffer, or coyote hunting, or fly through the sky, it's none of your business. I'll do what I please, and go where I like, and I don't need for you to run to my Daed or my uncle telling tales!"

Aaron's eyes were grim, but he replied: "I'm not running to anyone, Annie. I'm trying to keep the two of you from getting killed. Samuel is going to end up wrapped around a tree one day. You don't know it, but this isn't the first time he's nearly got himself killed!"

Annie scowled at him. "What are you talking about?"

"I mean that he totaled a buggy last year racing some other guy on the River Road. It was a miracle that he didn't break his neck, but the horse wasn't so lucky. It broke both its front legs and had to be put down. That's why he had to buy the black!"

Annie stared at him, open-mouthed, and Aaron nodded.

"Samuel has a right to risk his own neck, I guess," he told her, "but he doesn't have the right to risk yours, or other people's. If you're smart, Annie, you'll stay away from him."

Annie set her mouth. "I can choose my friends without your help, Aaron Graber!" she snapped.

"All right, Annie. I've said what I came to say," he retorted. "And your friends are your own business. But I'd hate to hear that you died of choosing the wrong ones."

On that Parthian shot, he stalked down the porch steps, but turned to add: "And what do you mean, go coyote hunting? No one is going to let a girl go on a coyote hunt, Annie. It's dangerous. What's wrong with you!"

Annie swelled with frustration, and on an evil impulse, swiped a handful of snow off the porch rail and smoked it at Aaron's head. The snowball hit him across the jaw with a satisfying *splush,* and made him give her a look that made her glad, momentarily, that he was sensible.

But she called after him just the same: "Looks like my aim is good enough for you, anyway, Aaron Graber!"

Aaron jumped into his buggy and drove away with a clatter, muttering angrily. After a minute or two the front door opened behind her, and her Daed drifted out onto the porch with a puzzled frown.

"What's going on out here, Annie? I heard your voices. They sounded almost angry."

"Aaron Graber thinks he's better than everybody else, and that he has the right to tell other people what to do." Annie cried. "I'm a better shot than he is, any day of the week, and I bet I'd bag more coyotes than him if I was only allowed. And it's nobody's business but my own which friends I choose!"

And to her father's astonishment, she ran back inside the house, and slammed the door behind her.

After a few minutes, Tim came out onto the porch and asked his father, with a frown:

"What's wrong with Annie? She's gone crazy! She's in the kitchen, cussing and tearing all the junk out of the drawers. I think she's actually going to clean something."

Mose shook his head. "I have no idea, son. But it was bound to happen sooner or later. Annie doesn't act like it, and we may have forgotten it, but she's a female. Once they reach Annie's age, it's no use to try to understand."

"But—"

Mose put a hand on Tim's shoulder and shook his head. "No, son. The sooner you learn it, the happier you'll be. Just nod and smile."

Tim looked back toward the house hopefully. "Do you think she might be mad enough to cook dinner?"

"We can always hope."

CHAPTER ELEVEN

Annie shifted her weight uncomfortably on the hard church bench and rolled her eyes to her uncle's. Her Uncle Joseph was standing in front of Silas Hershberger's huge upper room, delivering his Sunday sermon, and his glance made her shrink whenever it turned her way.

"We face too many dangers in the world right now, to court danger willfully. And it's selfish and wrong to endanger others," the bishop said solemnly, and heads bobbed in agreement all over the room.

Annie looked over at her Aunt Katie, who was sitting to her right. Her face was as placid as dawn. Beyond her, her daughter Emma regarded her father with perfect serenity, and even little Dorathea was beautifully behaved.

But Annie felt like she was sitting on a hive of ants, because she knew where her uncle was going with his sermon and wondered if he already knew that she'd been buggy racing with Samuel Stauffer.

And, more importantly, if he was going to mention it in church and make them confess in front of everybody.

She rolled her eyes to where Samuel Stauffer was sitting on the men's benches opposite. He was lounging there, all brushed and scrubbed and shiny as a new penny, and what was worse, he looked relaxed – as if he didn't have a care in the world.

Annie's eyes moved to Aaron Graber. He was sitting a few benches back but she could still see him, and to her annoyance, he was looking at her as if he were saying: *You know I'm right.*

Annie ground her teeth and couldn't figure which of them made her madder – Samuel, with his insane belief in his own luck, or Aaron, for being a rat and a meddler.

"I've been told that there's been more buggy racing on the roads around here," Joseph added grimly, sweeping the congregation with his bright eyes. "I'm disappointed to hear that some in this district may have been involved. And if they were, I expect the ones who did it, to come and confess."

There was shocked mumbling around the room. Annie rolled her eyes miserably to her uncle's, but to her relief, he wasn't looking at her.

But when she turned her head, Annie discovered to her dismay that Katie was. Her aunt's keen eyes were on her, as searching as two green spotlights. Annie gave her a sickly smile, and the most innocent look she could muster, and hunched lower down in her seat.

She glanced at Samuel's face. To her amazement, her accomplice in crime looked almost bored. He lifted his hand to his mouth, gnawed a hangnail briefly, glanced at it, sighed, and then gazed up at the bishop with a look of perfect innocence.

Even a smile.

Annie could feel a cat face coming on, and quickly lowered her eyes. Samuel Stauffer had done it again. He was going to be up in front of the whole church confessing his crimes, and he was going to drag her there with him. Her uncle had been right, it was all going to come out, and she was going to be up to her ears in trouble again.

"We've had too many deaths from buggy accidents," her uncle was saying, "and nothing is sadder than a funeral that didn't have to happen. I expect the person who was racing to come and confess. And if I have to find out about it from someone besides the people who did it, then it's going to go harder for them."

Annie looked at Samuel again. He straightened his legs out lazily, looked down at his shoes, moved his feet, looked up at the ceiling and then over at her – purely by chance, she was convinced.

Annie met his eyes grimly, and tried to put everything she was feeling into that glance, but Samuel raised his brows, smiled just a touch and looked down again.

Annie stifled an impatient expletive only by remembering

where she was, and she couldn't help shooting a worried glance toward Aaron Graber. He was still staring at her with that *significant* look, and Annie wondered how long she had before he cracked under the pressure and spilled everything he knew. She shook her head bitterly.

But Aaron's betrayal was more than just a problem.

It hurt. A lot.

She never would've ratted on Aaron, not in a million years, and she never would've believed that Aaron could rat on *her*. But she could tell by the way he was looking at her that she'd found the one thing that had snapped his twig.

Or rather, Samuel had found it.

Blast you, Samuel Stauffer, Annie thought bitterly, *I hope God sends a squirrel up your pants leg!*

Let us pray, her uncle was saying, and everyone bowed their heads, but to Annie's guilty dismay, her Aunt Katie's searching glance was on her again, as she closed her eyes.

"You worry too much, Annie!"

Annie glared up at Samuel Stauffer's twinkling eyes. She had finally managed to get him alone after lunch in a little alcove off the Hershberger's back porch. He leaned his hand up against the wall, and looked down at her.

"It was Aaron Graber who told, wasn't it?"

Annie scowled and turned her head, and Samuel laughed. "It *was* Aaron," he confirmed.

"I didn't say that!"

"You didn't have to. Your face is like a *sign*, Annie."

"Then what do you think my face is saying now?" Annie challenged him. "I'm in big trouble, because of you! Now we're both going to have to get up in front of the church, and confess."

"We're on rumspringa, remember?" Samuel laughed. "We don't have to confess anything unless we join the church. And Aaron's a decent guy. He won't tell, anyway."

"Don't be too sure," Annie grumbled. "He ratted us out, didn't he?"

"Not really," Samuel told her. "If he was going to name names, he would've done it at first. Aaron is sending me a message, Annie. This thing goes way back between us."

Annie was momentarily distracted from the main issue. "Then why didn't *I* know about it?" she demanded. "I know everything else about the two of you."

"I hate to break it to you, Annie, but sometimes guys don't tell their girl – their *female* friends – everything," Samuel laughed.

Annie narrowed her eyes. "It sounds like they're doing something they shouldn't, then."

Samuel sighed. "Last year I was racing one of Aaron's cousins on the River Road. I had a sweet little chestnut filly, fast as lightning, and Seth had a big bruiser of a horse that he was itching to race. He practically threw the money in my face. So I raced him."

He shook his head. "It wasn't my driving that caused the crash, Annie. It was Seth's mistake. He was driving with a worn harness and it broke. He lost control of his horse and it came right over on me. Seth and I came out all right, but the filly took the brunt of it."

He shook his head. "It broke my heart to have to put her down, but she was past saving."

"Aaron's right, Samuel," Annie told him. "You should stop racing. It's dangerous."

He looked down at her, in mild surprise. "Of course it's dangerous, Annie," he agreed, smiling. "That's why it's fun. And that's why we like it."

"We?" Annie retorted. "Don't lump me in with your craziness, Samuel. I'm done. From now on, you can ride in that buggy by yourself."

"Oh, come on, Annie," Samuel replied, "Admit it. If I'd driven like your granny the other day, you wouldn't have had near as good a time."

Annie scowled and looked away, and Samuel laughed. "You know it's true! You love excitement as much as I do."

"What I love is to wake up in the morning," Annie told him grimly, but he shook his head.

"No you don't, Annie. You're not like the other girls around here, and you never were. In fact, I'd lay five to one odds that you don't even stay. You're not going to make an Amish woman. It just isn't in you."

Annie sucked in air, because Samuel's shrewd observation hit too close to home. She raised her eyes to his with an almost frightened look.

Samuel was looking down at her, and his eyes were tender.

"No, Annie. You love to run, and to race, and to ride horses, and to speak your mind and be free. That just doesn't work around here, and especially not for a girl. You're going to have to choose. You *can* be free.

"Or you can stay here and be safe."

Then he leaned in and pressed his lips against hers in a soft, sweet kiss. Annie felt her heart jump in her chest, but she allowed Samuel Stauffer to take her in his arms and kiss her – not just once, but twice.

When he pulled away, Annie's eyes were glued to his.

"I hope you choose to be free, Annie," he whispered. "Because I sure mean to be."

Then he laughed again, pulled a little wisp of her hair out from her kapp, and walked back into the house.

Leaving Annie to stare out into the Hershberger's snowy yard with big, round eyes.

CHAPTER TWELVE

Aaron Graber pulled his buggy to a stop in Joseph Lapp's drive and jumped out into the snow. He slung a pack and a gun case over his shoulder. It was a fine, bright winter's day, and clear as a bell.

It was a good day for hunting.

Joseph's son Jeremy came walking out from the house and threw up his hand. "Hi Aaron. I'll take your horse out to the barn. Everybody's already inside."

"Thanks. You coming with us?"

Jeremy looked back at him as he unhooked the horse. He shook his head. "Not today. I have too much work to do here. Maybe next time. Get one for me."

"I will."

Aaron strode across the snowy lawn and climbed the steps. He paused on the threshold to stamp the snow off his boots, and then walked in.

Warmth, the smell of baking bread, and the cacophony of many people talking at once enveloped him. The living room was full of men talking. Most of them were already dressed in winter camo and hunting boots, like him. He saw the bishop and his oldest son, Hezekiah; Mose Miller and his son, Tim; Levi Zook and his sons; and Abe Beiler.

Joseph looked up at his arrival and called, "There he is! Sit down and grab a bite to eat, Aaron, before we go."

Aaron waved and turned into the kitchen. The bishop's wife and his pretty daughter, Emma, were busy at the stove. They had filled the table with platters of sliced ham and biscuits and baked cinnamon apples, and Aaron made himself a ham biscuit and sank down onto the bench to eat.

Emma walked over and pushed a bowl of gravy toward him. "Cup of coffee, Aaron?"

He nodded, and swallowed. "Thanks."

The bishop raised his hand suddenly and called for silence. "Let's pray before we go, and ask God's blessing on our hunt."

They all bowed their heads, and Aaron set his food on the table and closed his eyes. They prayed silently for a few moments, and then the bishop called:

"We're going to be driving over to Mark Hostetler's farm. He says we can leave our buggies there, and hunt on his land.

There have been lots of sightings there, and we think there's a den nearby.

"From there, we'll walk over to Thomas Miller's property and set up there for a few hours, and if all goes well, we'll move on to Adam King's pastureland. Are we all ready to go?"

There was renewed murmuring, and a general move toward the door. Mose Miller walked up and put his hand on Aaron's shoulder.

"Why don't you ride with us, Aaron?" he offered.

Aaron colored faintly, but nodded.

Men streamed out the door, talking and laughing and comparing notes. Aaron followed, carrying his gear, but he wasn't paying attention to what was being said.

He was still thinking of Annie, of how angry she'd been. He shook his head.

Maybe he shouldn't have told the bishop about the buggy tracks. Maybe he shouldn't have told Annie about Samuel's racing accident, either. In a sense, she'd been right, he had ratted them out. It would've made anybody feel betrayed.

And hurt.

But the way he saw it, he didn't have any other choice. Samuel was a skilled driver, and he'd been unbelievably lucky so far, but he was way past due for a reality check.

Aaron frowned. He just didn't want Annie to be there when Samuel finally got it.

He followed Tim into Mose Miller's old buggy and stowed his gear in the back. He saw that Tim was carrying Mose's old rifle – Annie's favorite. Aaron shook his head. That probably hadn't gone down well with her, either.

He looked up at Tim's freckled face. "How was Annie this morning?"

Tim grimaced. "*Crazy*. As usual! Still sulking about not being able to come with us."

Mose settled into the driver's seat, but at this, he turned around.

"Tim, I won't have you speaking disrespectfully of your sister. Annie might not be able to come on this trip, but if I catch you rubbing it in, it's the woodshed for you. You're not too old to take over my knee!"

Tim flushed, and Aaron lowered his eyes to hide the smile in them. But after awhile, a more serious mood took him. He looked up at Mose.

"Maybe we should've let Annie come along," he said quietly.

Mose looked back at him in surprise. "You heard what the bishop said, boy. The answer was no."

So Aaron had to drop it; but the mental image of Annie

curled up on her bed and crying, stayed with him all the way out to the fields.

They drove out to Mark Hostetler's farm and parked the buggies there. They assembled their gear in the yard as the Hostetler boys took their horses to his barn.

Then they walked out into his pastures, and out the back fence to the wilder, more wooded property, and beyond into the open fields. None of them spoke a word.

They fanned out a bit, and Aaron followed Mose as he crouched down behind an overgrown fence line and set up a rifle stand. The others found hiding places behind clumps of trees or scrub bushes and settled in.

Levi Zook was in cover behind a small outcrop of rock, and he lifted a hand call to his lips. A strange, wailing sound – the cry of a fawn in distress – went up into the air.

The sound echoed out over the fields.

Aaron scanned the snow and all the little dips and hollows in the land. There wasn't a sound, and not a flicker of movement anywhere. He frowned.

Coyotes were notoriously smart and hard to kill. They were wary animals, and if you used a call that other hunters had used before, you were usually busted, because the coys learned fast.

Levi lifted the call to his lips a second time, and the

unnerving sound shuddered on the air. Aaron crouched low and watched narrowly for any sign of life.

There were none.

Levi raised the call a third time, but the only movement was a sudden rush on the far side of the pasture, where a covey of birds had been startled from cover.

Aaron crouched down again and peered through his gun scope. He couldn't see a thing. He glanced over at Mose, and they exchanged a wordless look.

After trying for an hour with no success, they gave up on that spot and moved on to Thomas Miller's property, which was about a mile down the road. There was a small, frozen stream winding across the center of the pastureland, with scrub brush, rocks and trees around it, and coyotes had been seen coming down to drink.

They set up again at different points in the meadow, taking care to move stealthily and without noise. There was no sign of life except for the solitary birds that skimmed overhead in the winter sky.

Another man raised a call. It sounded eerily like a wounded puppy, and Aaron winced, remembering his dog.

There was no reply, no movement.

They watched the stream for another hour without luck. Once a couple of deer came down to drink, and Aaron nudged

Mose and grinned. It took self-control not to blow their cover, but no one fired a shot, and the deer eventually drank their fill and wandered away.

After an hour or so they gave up there as well and walked to Adam King's land. It was heavily wooded on the far side, with rolling pastures in between. They entered it one at a time, silently, and fanned out at different points along the top of a ridge that commanded a good view of the land below.

Aaron settled in behind a screen of scrub brush next to a big rock, and to his surprise, Joseph Lapp came over and took cover next to him. He grinned at Aaron's surprise.

They crouched down, watching. Joseph lifted a hand call to his lips and made a strange, shuddering call into the air – the howl of a coyote.

He paused and waited. For a few long moments there was nothing.

Then, without warning, loud, wailing howls spiraled up to the sky. First one, and then two, and then four and then six big coyotes rose from cover at the far end of the pasture and came running boldly across the snow. They were big, tawny, wolf-like creatures, and Aaron's heart jumped. He put his eye to the scope and drew a bead on a big red coyote trotting behind the leader with its tongue lolling out.

The coyote stopped, and Aaron took careful aim.

Then he squeezed the trigger, and the rifle jumped.

At the same instant there was a hail of loud *pops*, and coyotes dropped all over the field, one after another.

But when Aaron raised his eyes from the scope, to his intense disappointment, the big red one was loping away for the trees. He'd pulled the trigger too soon.

He rested his chin on the scope disconsolately. "Annie would've made that shot," he muttered, half to himself.

To his surprise, Joseph Lapp put a hand on his shoulder. He looked down at Aaron, and then out across the field. He replied quietly:

"I believe it. But if Annie were here, I know at least one young man who would be even more distracted than he is now, and who wouldn't have his mind on business.

"And when you're shooting, Aaron, you have to keep your mind on business – all the time."

Aaron looked up at him, thunderstruck. But to his embarrassment, Joseph Lapp was right. He *was* distracted.

He bit his lip.

The evidence was the red coyote, as it turned to give him one last look before trotting off to the safety of the woods.

CHAPTER THIRTEEN

"I'm so glad to hear that she's not...*challenged*," Cora Muller was saying. She was sitting on the couch in her brother's living room folding baby clothes. "It was such a sad thought!"

Katie exchanged a look with Emma, and they both bit back a smile.

"No, Annie was just covering for a friend when she climbed up on your roof," Katie explained. "She never really believed that the goat would cause your baby to be"—she bit her lip—"born ugly."

Cora stopped folding and frowned. "Was her friend challenged?"

Katie smiled openly, and replied, "That's a question. But I think he understands now, that he got hold of some bad information."

Cora pursed her lips. "Really, people should be more frank

with their children. She could've fallen off the roof. Or been murdered by that hateful goat! It showed its true colors the other day, Katie. It charged the poor baby when he was just standing in the yard!" Her eyes kindled in outrage. "The very idea!

"And even when Isaac locked the buck in the pen," Cora went on indignantly, "the hateful thing found a way to unhook the latch with its teeth, and when Isaac came out that evening, it was up on the roof again. It took him forever to get it down. He had to throw snowballs, and one of them missed and almost broke our bedroom window!"

Her sister-in-law stopped wiping the countertop and gave her a stricken look. "Oh, Cora, I'm so sorry – we didn't know that the buck was mean. We've never had any trouble with the doe. Dorathea drags it around like a rag doll and it's never so much as opened its mouth!"

"Oh, it's not your fault," Cora answered quickly. "You couldn't have known, you didn't have it that long. And the buck fooled us all for a while. It's a crafty, wicked animal!"

Katie and Emma exchanged another look, and Katie lowered her eyes.

"Yes, we saw your ad in *Die Botschaft*. We were wondering why you were selling it for such a low price," Katie replied.

"Isaac *hates* it," Cora nodded. "It peed on all his beautiful tools, and he thinks he's going to have to make new ones, because you can hardly get the smell out with an acetylene torch, and he can't stand to use them like they are.

"Isaac said that if no one buys the goat, he's going to sell it for meat!"

Katie rolled her eyes to Emma's again. "Oh, dear. Well, we'll spread the word that you're selling it. Maybe someone around here could use the buck for something."

"Yes, please do!" Cora replied, unrolling a towel with a *snap*. "The sooner it's gone, the better! It's a menace to Isaac Joseph as long as it's with us, and it's caused your poor niece a world of trouble!"

"Yes, it has," Katie sighed. "But Annie has bigger problems than those goats of hers. I'm concerned about her."

Cora calmed down somewhat, folded a little pair of pants and smiled at her sister-in-law fondly. "Oh, you're always fretting about someone, Katie."

Katie shook her head. "It's my responsibility to fret about Annie, now that Elizabeth's gone. Annie hasn't had anyone to show her how to do so many things. Imagine it – she's courtship age now, and she's only just learned about men and women. And that's only because I had to shame Mose into letting me tell her."

Katie sighed and shook her head. "He lets her run completely wild. In the summer, the poor thing lives in a treehouse like a squirrel. She goes hunting, she doesn't know how to keep house and she thinks of boys as her buddies."

Cora shot her a mischievous look, but said nothing.

"But what she needs most now, is to take some thought for how she looks," Katie worried aloud. "Annie's a very pretty girl, she's got a cute figure and beautiful eyes, but you never notice because her hair is flying out from under her kapp, and her dress is always torn, and those ragged stockings—"

Cora shook her head. "I'd never dream of going out in public that way," she shuddered, and Katie's worried look deepened.

"Maybe we can help Annie," she murmured. "Cora, you're always so neat and pretty. Would you be willing to come over next weekend? Annie will be here next Saturday. Maybe you could show her the little tricks you use to get around the *Ordnung*. The rules against makeup, anyway."

Cora placed a folded quilt into a pile on the couch. "You do what you have to do," she sighed, and then dimpled. "All right, Katie, for you. I'll bring Isaac Joseph too, when I come. At least here, he'll be safe."

"I knew I could count on you," Katie replied gratefully, and went over to sit on the couch and give her sister-in-law a gentle hug.

"I can't squeeze too hard these days, can I?" she teased, and Cora went pink. "Are you and Isaac hoping for a boy, or a girl?"

"Isaac says he's happy either way, but I don't believe him. I think he wants another boy. But I want a little girl," Cora replied promptly. "I remember how much fun I had dressing Dorathea after she was born."

Katie went warm with pleasure, remembering how it felt to hold her baby in her arms. "Yes, she *was* a little doll, wasn't she?" she murmured softly.

"She was the most beautiful baby I've ever seen," Cora smiled, "except for Isaac Joseph."

"Yes, except for Isaac Joseph," Katie agreed fondly.

"Our baby should come this fall, in late September or early October," Cora went on. "We think that if it's a boy, we'll call him Noah, after Isaac's grandfather, and if it's a girl"—she peeped up at her sister in law—"we'll call her Katie. After you."

Katie's startled eyes flew to Cora's, and the warm look in them made her melt. She put a hand over her mouth and looked over at Emma, who looked almost tearful.

"I don't know what to say!"

"Say okay," Cora giggled, and Katie looked down at her in astonishment.

"Oh, of course it's okay!" she cried, took Cora in her arms and laughed.

CHAPTER FOURTEEN

Later that evening, the hunting party made its way back to the Lapp farm with a half-dozen large coyotes to show for a day's worth of hunting. Cora had gone back home, but Katie, Emma and Dorathea were there to welcome the hunters home and to refresh them with hot coffee and a table full of good things to eat.

"Where's my dinner?" Joseph called out, and shrugged out of his camo jacket. "Where's my mug?"

Katie laughed and brought Joseph his big white mug full of steaming coffee, and he warmed his red hands on it before lifting it to his lips. "*Aaaah,*" he sighed. "I've been dreaming of this, all day!"

"How many bad coyotes did you get, Daed?" Dorathea asked, and put her arms up to her father's. He lifted her by the waist of her dress with one arm and set her on his hip. Dorathea wrapped her arms around her father's neck, and he turned to whisper: "*Six huge, wicked ones with big googly eyes and long teeth.* Would you like to *see* them?"

Dorathea's blue eyes widened in alarm. She shook her head, and hid her face in her father's neck.

"Now, don't frighten her, Joseph," Katie told him, smoothing a hand over her daughter's hair.

Joseph turned his head. "You aren't scared of those old coyotes, are you ladybug?" he asked her. "They're not going to hurt you. We'll make a rug out of them."

He winked at Katie, and she pursed her lips in exasperation. "You'll have her dreaming of them tonight," she told him.

Joseph turned to the other men, still holding Dorathea with one arm. "Everybody come and grab some dinner," he invited. "We have a big pot of beef stew and plenty of fried chicken and hot potato salad."

The table, the chairs and sofa in the living room soon filled up with hungry hunters. Katie and Emma made plates and passed them from hand to hand, and though the table had been filled with platters of food, those platters were quickly wiped clean.

"Where do you think we should hunt next?" Hezekiah asked. "I'd like to go with you next time."

Levi Zook took a big bite of fried chicken. "Why didn't you come this time?"

"Oh, Jeremy and I had to take care of the chores, plus we

promised to help Leon Byler move some furniture today. His mother-in-law is coming to stay with them."

Levi shook his head. *"Pray for him,"* he murmured, and the other men laughed.

Abe Beiler looked up with a twinkle in his eye. "You boys aren't so far away from getting mothers-in-law," he teased. Jeremy grinned, but Hezekiah went red to the roots of his hair.

"Some little girls will make calf eyes at 'em, and they'll be gone," he told Joseph, laughing. He turned to where Aaron was sitting, at one end of the table. "And Aaron, too – he's not too young! We'll see him shining up his buggy, by and by," he gibed, and the other men laughed.

Aaron's face went a little red, and he smiled and shrugged and said nothing. But he noticed that while Joseph laughed with the others, his bright eyes lingered on him after the others turned away. And that while his expression wasn't unkind, it looked just a shade worried.

Aaron lowered his eyes and put a forkful of potatoes into his mouth.

That evening, after everyone had gone home, and they had closed up the house and gone to bed, Joseph reached over and turned down the lamp on the bedside table. Darkness flowed over the bedroom, and the only light was the chilly white moon, sending out a faint glow as it rose over the eastern hills.

Joseph pulled up the quilt and put his arm around Katie, and she moved over to lie on his chest. She looked up at him, snuggled in, and ran her fingers through his chest hair.

Joseph kissed her ear. "You know, Katie, you might be right to watch out for Annie," he sighed.

Katie opened her eyes and looked up at him. "What do you mean?"

Joseph sighed. "I think Aaron Graber may be a little taken with her. He missed an easy shot today, and I think it's because he was preoccupied with Annie. I think he felt bad that she didn't get to come with us. "There may be a little romance percolating there."

Katie digested this in silence. After awhile, she murmured: "I know he's a friend of Annie's, but I haven't seen anything to suggest there's more to it than that. At least, not from her side. But I wouldn't be unhappy, if it were true. Aaron's a good boy."

She fell silent again. "Though I'm not sure I'm happy, that it's happening now. If it's happening. Annie's too young to be dating yet."

Joseph stirred. "She's sixteen. It's a little young for courtship, but not too young."

His wife shook her head. "For some girls, but not for Annie. Annie may be sixteen, but she knows nothing about being a young woman. Nothing, Joseph. She needs to go slow, *very* slow, and she needs a boy who has good sense and who's willing to be patient."

"I don't know," Joseph objected, yawning. "Annie always seemed to have a pretty level head, to me."

"I've been watching her for years, Joseph. Annie has only two speeds," Katie told her husband. "Dead stop, or flying. If she starts dating, she needs a responsible boy to level out those extremes."

"Aaron's a responsible kid."

"He *seems* to be."

Joseph opened an eye and looked down at her. "You're going to be a tough one, aren't you?"

"Very tough," Katie smiled. "But I have to say, Aaron Graber is a much better possibility than that other boy she runs with."

"You mean Samuel Stauffer." Joseph sighed deeply. "Now there's a kid who worries me. I don't know for sure, but I believe he was one of the ones who was racing the other day. Some of the kids around town have told me that they saw him out driving in that direction."

Katie frowned. "I think Annie may have been with him, too," she said unhappily. "It freezes my blood to think of her riding in a buggy race, but it's just the sort of thing she'd do. And you should've seen her face at church when you were talking about it. She can't hide anything, and she looked as guilty as sin."

"Well, you can't discipline a church member on the grounds of looking guilty," Joseph sighed. "And all three of them are on their rumspringa. So unless we get proof, or a confession, we'll just have to hope that nothing worse happens."

Katie settled deeper down onto his chest, uneasily. "Oh, Joseph, that's not good enough," she quavered.

He leaned down and kissed her. "I know, sweetheart. Let's pray."

CHAPTER FIFTEEN

Annie unhitched her buggy and walked Ginny out to her aunt and uncle's barn. She had been there enough times that she felt comfortable doing it herself, and her cousin Hezekiah hardly looked surprised when he looked up from his chores and saw her.

"Hi, Annie! You can put her over in the second stall."

"Thanks."

When she was done, she walked the well-worn path to the front porch and up the steps. The weather had taken a warmer turn, and the snow had mostly melted off the lawn. It was late February, and while spring wasn't there yet, it was on its way. A few of Katie's daffodils were already blooming.

She knocked on the door, and Katie's voice greeted her from inside.

"Come on in, Annie!"

Annie turned the knob and went in. The warmth of the room felt good after the brisk breeze, and she closed the door behind her. Katie was sitting in the living room with Emma, little Dorathea and Cora Muller. Katie turned to her and smiled.

"Come on in, Annie, don't be shy! You know my sister-in-law, don't you?"

Annie went red, since Cora Muller had little reason to think well of her after that humiliating episode with the goat, but she put the best face on it that she could. She smiled crookedly.

"Hi, Cora."

Cora dimpled prettily and held out a bowl as Annie approached. "They're caramel creams," she explained, and popped one in her mouth. "Like one?"

Annie grabbed a handful, and sat down on the couch next to her.

"We were having a discussion before you came in," Katie told her, with mock solemnity. "We were trying to decide which is more romantic: a trip to Pinecraft, or a trip to the mountains."

Annie looked at her in confusion. Ordinarily, she rated a hen party only slightly less tedious than a tooth extraction or a math test, but since her last meeting with Samuel Stauffer, her world had tilted on its side and was spinning backward. She was sure of nothing anymore. She tucked a little twig of hair behind her ear.

"I vote Pinecraft," Cora told her. "I was only ever in a cabin when I had Isaac Joseph, and it was during a snowstorm and in the middle of nowhere!"

Emma nodded. "I vote Pinecraft too."

"That's only because Daniel Gingerich says he likes the beach," Cora teased her, and Emma went pink and smiled shyly.

"Well, I vote the mountains," Katie added. "A cabin by a quiet stream, with just the sound of the water in the daytime, and the crickets at night. That would be so romantic."

"I vote the mountains too," Dorathea piped up.

"What about you, Annie?" Katie smiled. "Which would you like best?"

Annie lowered her eyes. "I don't know. I guess, the mountains," she mumbled. Her glance wandered to the door.

"I've been reading a romance that's set on the beach in Pinecraft," Cora sighed dreamily, stretching her arms up above her head. "It's so beautiful. They had just gotten married, and the man took his bride out into the ocean after midnight, and then they—"

She shot a quick look at Dorathea, and then at Annie, and then at Katie, and blurted: " …and then they prayed together and went back inside."

"You shouldn't read those silly things, Cora," Katie told her with a smile. "What real man ever behaves like that?"

Cora looked up at her, and her eyes were like big blue marbles. "Oh, Isaac does!" she said earnestly. "But sometimes I have to remind him. And I have to hide the books from him. He doesn't like them."

"That should tell you something," Katie replied gently.

"They're just so sweet," Cora giggled. "Isaac doesn't like them, because he says I expect him to do all the things in the book, and he says they're silly."

"He's right."

"Well, what's wrong with telling your wife that her eyes are like"—Cora closed her eyes—"*melting mirrors of beauty*, and *angel's tears*, and *agonizing pools of liquid love*?"

"Does Isaac ever say those things?" Emma asked breathlessly.

"No," Cora replied sadly, and then brightened. "But he *does* tell me that I have pretty eyes. If he would only be a little bit more creative, he'd be perfect!"

"I wish I had eyes like yours, Cora," Emma told her wistfully. "They're so pretty. You're lucky. You look beautiful naturally."

Cora giggled, and looked conspiratorial. "My little toe! Look." She pulled a small bottle out of her bag. "This is my peppermint oil. I've been telling Isaac my lips are chapped, but a little dab of peppermint oil makes them plump up, nice and full."

Annie sat up straighter and looked at the bottle more closely.

Cora scrounged in her bag. "Come over here, Emma. I'll show you."

Emma laughed nervously and went to sit beside Cora. Cora pulled another tiny jar out of her bag and opened it.

"You take a little swipe of petroleum jelly, and add just a tiny little drop of peppermint oil," she murmured. She opened the bottle and tipped it onto one finger.

"Now push your lips out."

Emma giggled and made a face like a fish, and Cora leaned in and painted the mixture over her lips. "See – just a little swipe. It's going to tingle a little, but it'll make your lips plump out nice and full."

Emma made a face. "Ew, it does tingle!"

"Turn around and let us see," Katie commanded, and Emma turned around and puckered.

"You know, your lips *do* look a bit fuller," Katie laughed. "Not too much, though – it's nice and subtle."

Annie tilted her head to get a better look. Sure enough, Emma's lips looked just a tiny bit swollen. She put a finger to her own lips, wondering how they'd felt to Samuel Stauffer, when he'd kissed her.

But she could only be sure of one thing. *His* lips had felt warm and soft and...*really* good.

A wave of shame surged over her, and Annie was immediately disgusted with herself. She, of all people, was in danger of turning into an empty-head – a goober.

But, try as she might, she couldn't stop thinking about Samuel, hoping that he'd kiss her again, so she could really make up her mind about it.

Katie smiled and chimed in: "When Joseph and I were courting, I used to bite my lips just before I saw him, to make them look red. And pinch my cheeks, so they'd look nice and rosy."

Emma rolled her eyes to Katie's and burst out laughing. "Katie, *really*?"

"Don't tell your father." Katie told her, with a twinkle.

Emma looked down at her hands, and then over at her mother. "I sometimes rub a thin little layer of flour over my brow, and on my nose, just before I see Daniel," she confessed. "It takes the shine off my skin."

"Oh, that's an old one," Cora laughed. "I use corn starch. It works better."

Dorathea dimpled and looked up at her mother. "Mamm, put some corn starch on me!" she cried, and stuck out her little chin. Her mother shook her head.

"No, no, ladybug," she murmured fondly. "We're keeping you little as long as we can. When you get a bit older, then you can have it."

She turned to give her niece a conspiratorial look. "When you get to be Annie's age, you can wear it."

Cora's laughing eyes fell on Annie. "Come over here, Annie, and let me do you," she invited, patting the cushion beside her. Annie went beet red, but she couldn't deny that she was also curious to see if the peppermint oil would work. She went and sat down on the couch beside Cora.

"Now pucker up," Cora laughed, and Annie scrunched her face into a knot, and stuck her lips out.

The front door opened just then, and Hezekiah walked in. The women in the living room looked up at him, and then burst out into wild giggling.

He looked a question at Katie, who quickly assured him: "Don't pay it any mind, Hezekiah. We're just having fun."

He smiled uncertainly and walked across the room, intensely conscious of five pairs of feminine eyes on him. He slowly climbed the first few steps on the staircase, and another burst of laughter broke out.

He looked back over his shoulder in consternation, but no one explained, and so he took the rest of the staircase two steps at a time.

CHAPTER SIXTEEN

"I have such a hard time braiding my hair."

Annie looked up into Katie's sympathetic eyes. "Most of the time I just twist it together and hope that it holds."

They were sitting on the little single bed in the guest room upstairs, the place where Annie always spent the night when she came to visit. Dinner was over, the dishes were washed and the children were in bed. It was the comfortable twilight hour, a time for winding down.

And for secret confidences.

Katie reached up and unpinned her own kapp, revealing a neat braided bun underneath. She set the kapp down on the bed and pulled out the pins holding her hair in place, and her long brown braids tumbled down around her shoulders.

"I'm going to do my own, and you can watch," Katie told her. "And then you can copy me. It isn't as hard as it looks. It just takes practice."

Annie's dubious face wasn't expressive of confidence, but Katie smiled and freed her hair from their braids with surprising speed. Then she reached into a drawer in the bedside table, pulled out a brush, and smoothed the rippling waves into a sleek, shining waterfall.

"Now, watch what I do," she commanded, and turned away from Annie. "You don't even need a mirror. You can do it by feel. I'll show you an easy shortcut at first, and then you can practice until you're ready to try the harder way."

Annie watched as Katie pulled her fingernail down her scalp, making a neat center part. Then she divided her hair into three equal parts, holding one skein in her left hand, and one in her right, like ponytails.

"Now watch. You just take the right bunch of hair, and cross it over to the middle."

Annie tilted her head to see.

"And then you take the left bunch of hair, and cross it over to the middle, too. And you pull it all *tight*, like so. Do you see how I'm doing it?"

Annie nodded. "I see."

"Then you just work it all the way to the bottom, like this, and then you tie it with a rubber band and pin it up on the top of your head, like *so*." She quickly fastened her hair back up in a neat, pretty coil.

"Now let me see you do it."

Annie took a deep breath and unburdened herself of her kapp. She took the brush and merely ran it through her loosely twisted hair, as pins rained down on the quilt. When she'd brushed it smooth, she tried to copy what Katie had done, slowly folding sections of her hair.

"Good, good," Katie approved. "Keep working each piece to the center, and then pull it tight. Now tie it off, and let's pin it up."

Annie coiled the thick braid on the top of her head, and stuck it with pins. She looked over at Katie.

Her aunt smiled, took her by the shoulders, and turned her toward a small mirror. "Look, Annie."

Annie raised her eyes to the mirror. A pretty young woman, with neat, shining hair and slightly pouty lips was staring back at her.

"See? You can be a beautiful young woman, Annie – if you make the effort."

Annie met her aunt's eyes in the mirror and blurted: "Aunt Katie, who was the first boy you ever kissed?"

Katie's brows rose in surprise. She gave Annie an amused glance.

"*Hmmm*…the first one. That would have to be John Muller," she replied. "He was a very handsome boy, let me tell you. All the girls were wild for him. Now, he's been married twelve years, and has seven children," she laughed.

"But *then,* he was tall and had dark hair and nice gray eyes. We went out a few times, and I liked him a lot. Until another boy came along and made me forget all about him," she laughed.

"When did John first kiss me?" she mused. "It was during harvest time, and his father had a big wagon, and so he let the kids get on it and have a hay ride one night," she murmured, staring out the window into the deepening twilight. "It was a beautiful night with a big harvest moon, and very warm." She sighed, and then seemed to come back to herself.

Annie smiled faintly. "Someone kissed me the other day," she confessed, in a small voice. "It was the first time ever, for me."

A tender look flooded over Katie's face, and she reached out and took Annie's cheek in one hand. "How was it then, Annie Miller?" she smiled.

The ghost of a smile played over Annie's face. "I liked it a lot," she confessed, and Katie laughed softly.

"Don't like it too much, *Miss Just Been Kissed,*" she whispered, and hugged her. "If I hear of a young man getting fresh with my niece, we're going to have big trouble," she teased, but the look in her eye told Annie that her aunt was only half joking.

"Oh, it was only a kiss," Annie assured her. "But...I didn't know what to do. I don't know *how* to kiss anybody."

"Don't be in a hurry to learn," her aunt told her softly. "You're very young, Annie. You have lots of time."

"I feel so...confused," Annie confessed, in a small voice.

"Of course you do, darling. That's normal."

Annie lifted troubled eyes to her aunt's face. "What do I do when I see him again?" she asked.

"Why, smile. And be nice to him," Katie suggested gently. "And be sure that you make it clear that you're a lady, and that you expect him to be a gentleman."

"Oh, I don't worry about that part," Annie muttered absently. "If he were to be stupid, I'd just slug him."

Katie burst out laughing, and pulled Annie into her arms. "You have my permission," she told her, with a twinkle. "If any boy gets *stupid* with you, you pull back and slug him, right across the nose!

"But if *not,* then I recommend you just be nice to him."

She pulled back, and rose. "It's getting late, and we have to get up early tomorrow. I'll let you get to bed now."

Annie stood up and hugged her shyly. "Thank you, Aunt

Katie," she whispered. "I mean it, thank you."

"Sweet dreams, darling," Katie smiled, and softly pulled the door closed behind her.

But when she reached the end of the long hall, turned the corner and opened the door to her own bedroom, her husband crossed his arms behind his head and nodded toward the other end of the house.

"Are you coming to bed, at last?"

"Oh now, Joseph," Katie chided, and sat down at her dresser. "It's an important time for Annie." She turned to look at him, unpinning her kapp. "She told me that a boy kissed her for the first time."

"*Hmm*. So there is something going on between her and Aaron Graber."

"It looks that way."

"Is there any hope that something might go on between you and your sad, lonely husband?"

Katie turned to face him. "There might be."

Her husband's smile faded somewhat as he stared at her. "Did something happen to your mouth, Katie?" he asked, frowning.

"No. Why do you ask?"

"It's just that your lip looks a little swollen, that's all."

CHAPTER SEVENTEEN

On Monday morning, Daniel Gingerich pulled up to the front of the Miller house to drive Annie in to work. But when the door opened, and Annie came running out, he had to look twice to credit his own eyes.

The girl who came running down the steps to the buggy was a stranger.

Her hair was neatly pinned into a tidy braid on the top of her head, and covered by a clean, intact, correctly positioned kapp. Her cape was in decent repair, and her stockings – wonder of wonders! – had not one rip or moth hole.

Daniel leaned forward. "*Annie?*"

She climbed up into the buggy and settled into the seat beside him. "Let's go, we'll be late," she told him breathlessly.

Daniel stared at her face in amazement. There was something different about her face, too, though he couldn't quite put his finger on it. She looked healthier, maybe.

"What did you do to yourself, Annie?" he blurted. "You look almost—" He bit his lip at the last minute, but to his relief, Annie didn't flare up at his tactlessness.

"Come on," she urged, and so Daniel turned to the horse. "Get up," he murmured, and shook the reins.

But all the way to the store, Daniel Gingerich had to bite back a smile. Because no matter what had caused it, one thing was as clear as day: in spite of all her teasing, Annie Miller had finally decided to join the rest of the world.

By 9 a.m., the two of them had the store open and ready for business. Annie helped Daniel open the boxes of spring inventory and began to clear out most of the store's winter items. They filled the shelves with garden paraphernalia, a new line of Amish cookbooks and some baked goods from local suppliers: loaves of fresh bread, pies and cupcakes.

At about 10 o'clock, Emma dropped by to bring them an order of her friendship bread. And for the first time ever, Annie decided to show mercy and went outside to let Emma and Daniel talk to each other in private.

While she was standing there, a buggy rolled into the gravel lot, and Annie shaded her eyes with one hand.

To her embarrassment, it was Aaron Graber.

Annie looked down at her shoes, not knowing whether to

stand her ground or to go back inside; but she finally decided that it would be stupid to run from her friend, even if she was mad at him. She crossed her arms and waited for him to climb down from his buggy.

Aaron put a hand through his dark hair, and squinted at her in the morning sunshine.

"Hi, Annie."

Annie turned her head and looked off into the trees. "Hi."

"Look, Annie, I came over to make peace with you. I know you're mad at me, but it's silly to fight."

"You stabbed me in the back, Aaron Graber," she told him with an angry glance. "And Samuel, too! I would never have done that to you, and neither would he."

"It had to be said, Annie."

Annie turned to him, eyes flashing. "Why? Nothing happened!"

"No, thank God." Aaron retorted, "But it could have, and you know it. If Samuel keeps on pushing his luck, one day his luck is going to run out!"

"I'm working. I don't have time to stand here talking to you," Annie began, but Aaron stepped up and put a hand on her arm.

"Let go of me!"

Aaron removed his hand, but the pained sound in his voice compelled Annie better than any physical restraint.

"Annie, do you think I took any pleasure in telling your uncle?" he objected. Annie pulled her mouth into a straight line and tried to meet his eyes, but to her own annoyance, the truth in them made her drop her glance.

"I know you, Annie. I knew you'd be as mad as fire. But some things are more important than always getting along."

"Well, congratulations, then," she snapped, "because we *aren't*." The sound of an approaching buggy made her lift her eyes, and an angry smile dawned over her face.

"You can offer your apology to Samuel, if you want to," she told Aaron briskly, "because here he is."

The gleaming gray buggy came rolling up to the lot and pulled in beside Aaron's. The glorious black snorted and tossed his head, and Samuel grinned and leaned out of the window.

"Morning, Annie! Morning, Aaron!"

"Hello, Samuel," Aaron replied.

"Hey Annie, it's a beautiful morning!" Samuel called. "Care for a drive?"

Annie threw an angry glance over her shoulder at Aaron. "I'd *love* one!" she replied, and Samuel extended his hand. Annie ran over, took it, and jumped up into the seat. Within seconds, Samuel had backed the buggy around and was disappearing down the road at a brisk clip.

Aaron watched them go with a grim expression, and then lifted his eyes and his hands to the sky, as if he was appealing to God.

CHAPTER EIGHTEEN

Samuel Stauffer turned to look at Annie as they rolled down the road in the springlike sunshine. His blue eyes sparkled, and his teeth did, too.

"You're as pretty as a picture this morning, Annie Miller!" he blurted, and then laughed. "Springtime agrees with you! Or can I hope that *I* do?" he teased, and Annie lowered her glance and went red.

"I'm going ziplining this morning," he added casually, and Annie rolled her eyes to his hopefully.

"Wanna come with me?"

Annie squirmed – pleased, but doubtful. "I can't go ziplining in a dress," she objected, and Samuel nodded. "See that duffel bag in the back? I brought a pair of English tees and pants for us. That is, if you dare to wear them."

Annie bit back a shocked smile. She'd never worn English

clothes before, but Samuel made it sound as easy as falling down.

"Well, what do you say?"

"Well...I'm supposed to be working today," Annie demurred, but Samuel waved the objection away. "Oh, Daniel can get along without you for a day," he told her, and Annie smiled slowly.

"Oh...okay," Annie grinned, and nearly hugged herself in glee.

Samuel drove the buggy along the back roads, through farmland that gradually began to roll in gentle hills, and then climbed to bluffs and mountainous foothills.

"We're going to Fern Mountain," he told her, as they began to climb a long, steep slope. "I've been there twice before, and it's a blast. There's one descent that shoots you down the side of the mountain at more than 50 miles an hour!"

Annie's nervous system sparkled and popped with a sensation like an electric shock. Even the idea of that much speed excited her, and Samuel looked at her and laughed.

"You like the sound of that, don't you, Annie?" he teased. He leaned over suddenly and gave her another kiss, right on the mouth, and Annie raised her brows in surprise. But to her delight, the feel of Samuel's lips was just as lovely as it had been the first time.

When they arrived at the entrance, Annie leaned out of the window and looked up in anticipation. The ticket office was a plain brown box with a few outbuildings all around and what looked like a garage to one side.

But when she raised her eyes, she could see wooden towers dotting the hills behind, with long, high lines connecting them a good 30 feet above the ground. Her hands and feet began to tingle in anticipation.

Samuel parked the buggy in front of the office, tied up, and extended a hand to Annie.

"Come on!"

Annie smiled, turned to grab the duffle bag, and jumped out to join him.

Once inside, Samuel went to buy their tickets, and Annie walked to the restroom. She found it to be a very basic space made of particle board siding, fitted with a grungy sink and toilet, and lit by one bare lightbulb. But there was an empty chair by the door, and she put the bag in it and began to undress.

She opened the duffel. Samuel had chosen a white tee shirt and a pair of blue drawstring pants for her. By English standards, they were conservative clothes – the tee was a simple scoop neck with short sleeves, and the pants looked roomy and comfortable.

But by Amish standards, they were scandalous.

Annie chewed her lip and stared at the tee in doubt. Her arms would be *bare*, and so would her neckline.

But it was her rumspringa, after all – and no one but Samuel would ever know.

She reached up and pulled off her kapp and placed it carefully in the bag, and then unpinned her shining braids. They rippled down to her waist like coppery ribbons.

Annie looked at herself in the dusty mirror. The girl looking back at her was actually kind of cute. She smiled at her own reflection, and quickly finished dressing.

When she walked out again, Samuel was talking to the cashier, but he turned his head briefly when she approached.

And froze.

His brows twitched up, and his lower lip fell down – just a tiny bit. His hands froze in the air.

Annie felt herself going warm, because even *she* understood that look. She smiled at him, and twirled around.

"What do you think?"

Samuel blinked, and smiled. "Annie, you're... *really pretty.*"

"Here's your tickets."

Samuel came to himself, smiled at her again, and took the tickets from the cashier. "I'll be right back," he told her, and grabbed the duffel bag as he passed.

When he emerged again, ten minutes later, it was Annie's turn to be pleased. Samuel's bright blonde hair shone like corn silk under a plain baseball cap, and he'd chosen a blue tee shirt and a pair of jeans.

Annie pursed her lips and felt another wave of heat crawl up from her feet to her hair. She felt very wicked, but she couldn't help but notice how those clothes showed off Samuel's body. His arm muscles bulged out of the tee shirt sleeves, and his stomach was as flat as a board.

She felt herself going red, but when Samuel held out his hand, she took it.

Their driver soon appeared. He was a young, tan English boy who motioned them to follow him. He led them out to the parking lot, where an open-topped jeep was idling. He jumped into the driver's seat, and they followed.

Annie saw Samuel's eyes moving hungrily over the hood, and she knew the thought in his mind. He was already wondering how fast it would go.

And they both soon found out.

The driver gunned the motor, and the jeep bounced away over the rocky hillside, following no road that Annie could see except a bare footpath that crossed a pasture, dived down into a creek and then across it, and then surged up a near-vertical hill. The jeep slammed them from side to side as it went swaying drunkenly up the incline, and Annie had to grab the metal door more than once to keep herself from being tossed right out onto the ground.

"The first tower is on the very top of the mountain," the driver shouted over the roar of the motor, as they crashed through a wall of underbrush and surged up a narrow, rocky road. "It's the longest zipline in the course, more than a thousand feet from top to bottom."

Samuel looked back at her and smiled, and Annie felt her mouth go a little dry with excitement. She looked up through the trees, and the base of a massive wooden tower was just visible through them.

The jeep burst through the underbrush and emerged onto a flat, graveled space at the base of the tower. The driver parked the jeep and beckoned to them to follow as he climbed a steep flight of wooden stairs. There was another boy standing at the top.

Samuel took her hand, and they climbed the tower together. When they reached the top, Annie inhaled sharply. She could see the tops of trees far below their feet, marching all the way down the mountainside, and the blue foothills stretched out beyond, all the way to the misty horizon. It felt like the top of the world.

She turned to Samuel, her eyes wide with wonder.

He looked at her fondly and squeezed her hand. "It's beautiful, isn't it, Annie?" he replied softly.

"Now, Tom is going down first," their guide explained. "He'll be there to stop you at the bottom."

The boy hooked himself into a padded harness, pulled down on it once, and threw himself off the edge of the platform. Annie watched, open-mouthed, as he zoomed down the singing line like a bullet, and then bounced up and onto his feet at the bottom.

"Who wants to go next?"

"I will. Hold my hat, Annie." Samuel pressed his baseball cap down on her head and grinned. Annie cast another glance down the steep mountainside at the tiny figure waiting far below.

The guide helped Samuel into his harness, checked it, and then gave him a thumb's up. To Annie's horror – and delight – Samuel tucked his head under and flipped as he jumped off the ledge, and flew – upside down, and kicking his feet in the air – all the way to the bottom.

Annie and the English boy laughed together to see him go. Then her guide turned to her and held out the harness.

Annie allowed him to hook her up in it. Her heart was thrumming with excitement.

"Don't grab the wire. And remember to keep your feet and arms pulled in," he told her. "Are you ready?"

Annie smiled and nodded, and without further ado, the boy

pushed her off the edge of the tower.

Annie slid off the edge and instantly went rocketing down the wire, flying like a bullet 30 feet above the ground. She screamed at the top of her lungs and clutched the harness rope with both hands.

No one had told her that it swiveled!

The world spun round and round and round as she went hurtling down the wire. The slender line hummed and vibrated as she gathered speed, and when she dared to open her eyes, Samuel and the other boy were rushing up with shocking suddenness.

The next thing she knew, she was bouncing high up in the air, and down again. The English boy grabbed the harness rope and pulled her to the ground.

"How'd you like it, Annie?" Samuel teased her.

Annie's heart was in her throat, but she rolled her eyes to his and shrieked with laughter, like a crazy thing.

"Let's do it again!" she cried.

CHAPTER NINETEEN

By mid-afternoon, Annie and Samuel had thrown themselves off a grand total of six zipline towers: the long one off the top, the one over the rock slide, the one through the pine thicket, the one running through the center of an empty barn, and the one they called the Kiss It Goodbye, with a terrifying drop straight down the side of the mountain. They finished up with the line that ran low over the lake – and the water fountain that was programmed to squirt up unpredictably. Samuel had gotten caught by the fountain, and Annie laughed until she cried when it blasted him right in the slats.

"*Ach!*" he'd cried, shaking out his sodden jeans leg, "the water's ice cold!"

But Annie had laughed until Samuel sputtered, and finally cracked up himself.

Back at the main office, they took turns with the duffel bag to change back into their usual clothes, and Samuel bought a photo for Annie – the one that showed her flying over the lake, her mouth wide with laughter and her braids flying.

And when they finally climbed back into the buggy, to Annie's delight, Samuel moved over and let her take the reins.

Her eyes moved quickly to his. "Really, Samuel?" she stammered.

He grinned at her. "Sure, Annie. You've earned your wings today!"

Annie settled into the driver's seat and shook the reins hard, and the black scrambled off over the parking lot, and down into the road. She kept the black well to the right, because the area got a lot of traffic; but when they'd gotten a little distance away, and turned off onto the smaller roads, Annie picked up the pace.

The black held its head up and went trotting down the road at a fast clip, his inky haunches shining like silk in the sun.

"Oh, go ahead, Annie," Samuel told her, in mock exasperation, "open him up. I can see you're dying to!"

Annie's eyes widened in excitement, and she leaned forward and bounced the reins off the black's back. "Get up!" she cried, and the black snorted and broke out into a run.

They went flying over the road, almost, it seemed to Annie, as fast as a car, and she laughed aloud. She suddenly felt that she knew why Samuel loved racing his buggy. It was the feeling of flying, of being free and powerful and alive.

It was how the hawk had looked – the one she'd seen flying in the sky. And it was how she'd felt when she'd gone flying down the mountain – as if she'd been a bird herself.

The road curved sharply, and Annie turned the black as smoothly as if she'd been using a steering wheel. Samuel nodded approvingly. "You're a good driver, Annie," he smiled. "It isn't easy to control him on a curve at this speed."

Annie tried not to let him see how much his compliment meant to her, but it pleased her. She stole a glance at Samuel's profile as she drove. Lately, Samuel's compliments pleased her more than they probably should.

Once they got back into town, Samuel made her take the buggy through a drive thru, and they ate sloppy hot dogs in the cab. Samuel let her have a bite of his slaw dog, and she gave him a sip of her orange drink, and they laughed and horsed around and had a generally great time.

Annie noticed some of the local kids staring at her as she drove Samuel's buggy through town, but this time she didn't care. She'd settled the matter in her own mind.

She'd decided that Samuel Stauffer had the right to be whatever he pleased – even a goober.

Because she'd decided that she liked him, after all.

And that she had the right to be a goober, too, if she wanted.

When she finally pulled into the parking lot of her father's store, Samuel stopped the buggy and turned to her. He put his hands over hers.

"I'm glad you came with me today, Annie," he smiled, and pulled a little twig of her hair out from under her kapp.

"It was a blast," Annie replied, looking steadily into his eyes.

"I knew you'd love it," he murmured, and then moved in for a kiss. Annie raised her lips to meet his, and smiled. She'd decided that she loved kissing Samuel, just as she loved ziplining and driving fast, and for much the same reason.

It was exciting.

Annie gathered her nerve, lifted her hands and dared to touch Samuel's blond hair. Then she sent tentative fingers exploring all through it. His hair felt thick and silky soft under her fingers.

Samuel curved his arms around her and pulled her close, and then gave her a new kind of kiss, much bolder, a kiss that made her nerves sparkle and pop like they had when she'd jumped off the mountain. Annie closed her eyes and allowed herself to feel that kiss.

It was thrilling.

And on a wild impulse, she pulled back from him suddenly, tilted her head, and nipped Samuel Stauffer's ear smartly between her teeth.

"*Ow,* Annie!" Samuel yelped. "What the—"

But Annie didn't reply. She vaulted out of the buggy and fled into the store without an explanation, a farewell, or a backward glance.

Samuel put a hand to his throbbing ear, and frowned: but after a minute or two, his expression lightened, and he chuckled to himself as he took the reins.

"*Little bobcat,*" he muttered, and laughed.

CHAPTER TWENTY

Annie linked her hands around her knees and sat on her sleeping bag, watching the stars from her treehouse. It was deep night, and a thick mist was rising from the distant meadow.

Faint moonlight slanted across the treehouse floor. It was a spring night, and still a bit chill, but not too cold to sleep outside. Far below, in the meadow grass, the first crickets of the season tuned up their solitary fiddles and played to her.

Annie rested her head on her knees. She hardly knew how to feel. She'd had a great day, one of the best days of her life, really. It had been so much fun, it had been dangerous and exciting and happy and…

She sighed, and frowned. But she still felt like a fool.

Samuel Stauffer probably thought that she'd lost her mind, to bite him like a dog when all he wanted was a kiss. She shook her head. She hadn't the first idea of how to be with a boy; she didn't know what to say or how to act. She just did whatever she felt like at the time.

Even if it was crazy.

She wondered if Samuel would think she didn't like him now, or if he'd just assume that she'd lost her mind.

Probably, that she'd lost her mind.

Annie thought of her mother's picture in the chest. She scooted over and picked the photo out of her scrapbook and brought it back into the moonlight. Her mother's smiling face was dim, but she knew it by heart anyway, every line.

How do you know if you're in love? Annie questioned her mother's smiling face silently. *Because I'm feeling lots of things. But I don't know what they are!*

When did you first know that you loved Daed?

How did you know?

Aunt Katie says that I have time. But I want to know the answer right now!

I wish you were here.

Annie looked down at the floor. The photo that Samuel had bought for her was lying there. She intended to add it to her scrapbook because she wanted to hold on to how happy she felt.

She looked forlornly out across the meadow, wondering if

Samuel was happy too, or maybe it was just another day for him.

He'd driven right past her aunt's house with another girl on the day of her last birthday party.

Annie sighed. She didn't even know who the girl was, or if Samuel might still be seeing her. At the time, she hadn't cared what Samuel did, or who he saw.

But she cared now.

A faint smile played across her lips. She was pretty sure she'd rung Samuel's bell at least once that day, though. The look on his face had been pretty funny when he saw her wearing those English clothes.

It made her want to wear English clothes again, and to fix her hair nicely, and maybe go beyond cornstarch and peppermint, and even get a little makeup –   except she didn't have any idea of how to wear makeup.

But she was sure of one thing: she wanted to make Samuel look at her that way again – like she was pretty. And to kiss her like he had that afternoon, with his whole mouth, like she was a peach and he was a starving man.

She hugged herself and smiled.

Daniel had given her a long lecture when she'd come back to work. He'd reminded her that they had to stock for spring, and that they'd been set back a day because she'd run out and spent the day playing. He told her that her Daed was counting on her to help, and that if she didn't do it, she was slacking off the job.

But he'd relented at last, and promised not to tell her Daed that she'd been out with Samuel, as long as she didn't do it again.

Annie smirked. That was probably because she had too much on him: Daniel had wasted more time talking to Emma than she'd ever thought about spending with Samuel.

But even so, deep down, Daniel was a sport.

Still, Annie wondered if she'd have the self-discipline to refuse if Samuel came to the store again with another offer of fun. It was hard to turn him down when she knew that she was going to have a blast.

Her thoughts returned briefly to Aaron and her argument with him. Her brow wrinkled into a troubled frown. Maybe she shouldn't have been so hard on him. Aaron was all right. He didn't mean any harm, she knew.

He was just too strait-laced, that was all. And he was probably still mad at Samuel because his cousin had been in that racing crash. But that hadn't been Samuel's fault.

That was hard to tell Aaron since he had a relative involved. Naturally he'd be on his cousin's side.

Annie yawned and stretched. It was late, and she was tired.

She decided to let it all go until tomorrow. She put her mother's photo on the floor beside her pillow, and crawled into the sleeping bag. The soft sound of the crickets gradually drove Aaron, Daniel, and the store and her job right out of her thoughts.

But Samuel Stauffer's twinkling blue eyes still danced before her, and his laughter floated in her ears; and she followed that sound away from the waking world, all the way into her dreams.

CHAPTER TWENTY-ONE

"He's still young, and he's strong and in good health. I've had him checked."

Isaac Muller stood in front of the goat pen, staring down at the buck. Ezekiel Yoder stood beside him, stroking his beard doubtfully.

"Why is there such a big lock on the pen?" he asked, squinting at the heavy metal catch.

Isaac glared at the goat. "He found a way to unlatch the first one with his teeth. I guess that means he's smart. But we have to watch him."

Ezekiel glanced up at Isaac's face. "Why are you selling him so soon after buying him?"

"He tried to butt the baby. So we can't keep him."

"Mean, eh?"

Isaac's face looked grim. "You could say that."

Ezekiel stuck his chin out and looked the buck up and down. "Well, the price is more than fair. And I don't care if he's mean. A stud only has one job, and if he does it, he'll be worth the price." He nodded. "I'll take him."

"Good. I have a crate in the workshop, and you can carry him home in it. I'll get it for you."

Isaac walked briskly to the workshop, and reappeared almost immediately, carrying it.

"I'll put him in the buggy for you."

"I appreciate that."

Isaac opened the pen, strode to the buck, and grabbed it unceremoniously by the horns. He twisted its head, dragged it to the crate, and pushed it in. There was a thunderous, *thumping* sound inside, but Isaac slammed the lid and locked it shut. He lifted it up in his arms, and carried it out to Ezekiel's buggy, and pushed it into the back.

There was a loud *bam* from inside the crate, and the box shook.

Ezekiel walked over and counted out a few bills into Isaac's hand. "Here's your money. Thanks for putting him up for me."

"My pleasure," Isaac told him, and waved as Ezekiel climbed up into the buggy and pulled out of their drive.

After he'd gone, Cora opened the door and walked out across the yard.

"Did Ezekiel buy the goat?" she asked.

"Yes," her husband answered, in a tone of deep relief. "It's gone at last!"

"I'm so glad!" Cora exclaimed. "I only hope it doesn't do poor Ezekiel a mischief!"

"Well, we don't have to worry about it anymore," Isaac told her, and put an arm around her waist. "I feel like a big rock's been rolled off my shoulders!"

"Come inside, and we'll celebrate," Cora suggested. "I'll make us a little cake, Isaac – a *'The Goat is Gone'* cake!"

Isaac smiled down at her. "That sounds good to me! No more goat!"

"Thank You, Lord!"

Later that afternoon, Emma walked across the meadow and up the hill to her young aunt's front door. She knocked softly, and Cora's voice called from inside.

"Come in, I can't get to the door!"

Emma opened the door to be greeted by the sight of Cora wrestling a wiggling Isaac Joseph. He was lying on the sofa, and she was trying to get him into his little shirt, but he was giggling and squirming.

"Stop wiggling, Isaac Joseph!" Cora laughed and broke up giggling. She turned to Emma. "See how much work I get done – I can't keep his clothes on. He will run out into the yard and pull them all off! Now calm down, baby, and let Mamm put on your shirt."

"Here, I'll hold him," Emma offered and sat down on the couch beside her. Between the two of them, they soon had Isaac Joseph fastened up.

"Oh, thank you Emma," Cora gasped and fell back against the couch. "He can run now, and he's faster than I am!" She set him down on the floor, and he smiled and climbed up into his Daed's big chair.

"I hope he behaves himself when we take him over to Naomi Zook's this afternoon," Cora laughed. "We have a play date, but she has a little daughter. The baby might give her too much information!"

"I haven't seen Naomi in months," Emma smiled. "It hasn't been as easy to get together since she married Nathan and moved to the edge of the district."

"I miss her," Cora sighed and folded up the baby's pajamas. "We used to play together as children. Her family lived next door to my parent's house, and we used to lie on the grass in the summertime and look up at the clouds and dream about who we were going to marry when we grew up."

Emma gave her an amused look. "Who did *you* think you were going to marry?" she teased.

"Oh, I couldn't decide," Cora giggled. "But Naomi always told me it would be Isaac. She could see it, and I couldn't!"

"What are you going to do when you go?" Emma asked.

"Oh, just let the children play in the yard, while Isaac and I catch up with Nathan and Naomi," Cora smiled. "Maybe I'll let Isaac Joseph run off all that energy. He's too much for me today!"

"Well, I won't stay long," Emma told her. "I just wanted to bring back the book you loaned me." She pulled a brightly-colored book out of her bag and gave it to Cora.

Cora looked back toward the stairs and giggled. "I have to keep it out of sight," she confessed. "But wasn't it good?"

Emma nodded. "I loved it," she sighed. "Maybe Daniel will take me to Pinecraft. If he ever proposes," she added shyly, and Cora laughed.

"He'd better, or I'll be mad at him," she replied.

Emma rose to go. "I'll see you later, Cora. Tell Isaac I said hello. Is he going with you?"

"Yes, he's out hitching up the buggy, and he's probably wondering where I am." Cora sighed, and turned to get Isaac Joseph. She was obliged to wrestle him out of his father's chair and to grab him by the hand to keep him from running away.

"Pray for me!" she cried, in mock distress, and Emma laughed.

CHAPTER TWENTY-TWO

Samuel Stauffer's shiny gray buggy glided to a stop in front of the Miller farmhouse at a little before noon. It was a windy day, with fluffy white clouds scudding across the blue sky, and every swaying branch was tipped with green. Samuel jumped down from the rig, tied up, and took the porch steps two at a time.

He leaned in and knocked jauntily at the door. After awhile, it opened to reveal Mose Miller.

"Why hello, Samuel," Mose murmured. His brown eyes held a touch of surprise. "What can I do for you?"

"I've come by to see if Annie might want to go for a ride in my buggy," Samuel answered. "It's a beautiful day for a drive."

Mose looked up briefly. "Yes it is." There was a long, heavy pause, and finally he added: "I'll go see where she is."

He closed the door again, and Samuel stood there waiting. After a minute or two, Annie appeared in the door. She smiled at him big and bright, and his confidence surged.

"Wanna go for a spin, Annie?"

Her face lit up with pleasure, and Samuel bit back a smile. Annie couldn't hide her feelings if she tried. Not that he wanted her to hide them.

Mose came back to the door. "How long do you plan to be gone, Samuel?" he asked.

Samuel looked up at him gravely. "Oh, only an hour or two, at most," he promised.

Mose leaned forward and squinted. "Why…what happened to your ear, boy?" he murmured, adjusting his glasses.

Samuel hunched his shoulder up and tilted his head. "Um – nothing. I just – got it caught in something."

"*Ah*," Mose replied, but he kept looking, and Samuel turned away quickly. "We'll be back in a little while!"

Mose nodded. "Be careful," he called after them, and stood watching with a troubled frown until they disappeared inside and drove away.

Once they were out of sight of the house, Samuel laughed and turned to Annie. "Well, how do you like it, Annie?" he teased and tilted his head so she could see the four perfect tooth marks on his ear lobe. "Behold your handiwork. It's lucky your Daed didn't get a closer look."

Annie slid down a little in her seat and went red. "I-I'm sorry, Samuel," she mumbled. "I don't know why I did it. I guess it hurt, huh?"

"Oh, only a little," Samuel told her lightly. "I'm used to it. It's not the first time I've been bitten by a woman."

At this, Annie frowned and turned her eyes to his. That sounded like one of Samuel's whoppers, but even so, she didn't like the sound of it.

"Who's been biting your ears, then, Samuel Stauffer?" she demanded, and he grinned.

"Oh, *this* one and *that* one. You don't know everything about me, Annie Miller."

Annie scowled and hunched down in her seat with her arms crossed. "I don't have to know anything about you," she mumbled, and Samuel laughed outright.

"Oh, don't flare up, Annie," he told her smugly. "Remember, jealousy is a sin!"

At that, she sat up straight. "Jealousy?"

"I just mention it, you know."

"I don't care who you run with, Samuel Stauffer—" she

began, but when she turned to glare at him, he just leaned over and kissed her, square on the mouth. His lips tasted of cinnamon, and they were soft and warm and delicious.

Then Samuel turned his jaw just a fraction, and told her: "Here's the other one, Annie. You can make it a match set."

Annie sputtered in spite of herself, and before she knew it, she cracked up laughing. Samuel was so full of bluff, she couldn't stay mad at him.

And lately, he was doing everything he knew to make her happy.

She had to admit, it was working.

"Here, Annie, take the reins," he offered, handing them to her. "Go easier today, though."

Annie took the reins gladly, and sent the black dancing down the road. It was a fine, warm spring day, with little traffic.

"Where do you want to go?" she asked him.

"Let's go out to the county line, to Silver Lake," Samuel suggested, reaching for his sunglasses. "It's a pretty drive this time of year."

Annie nudged the black, and they went rolling through the spring sunshine along the country roads. They passed another buggy occasionally, a neighbor who threw up a hand in passing, or maybe an English car zoomed past, and then Annie would have to hold the reins tight, because the black didn't like them; but he behaved beautifully for her, and kept a fast, steady pace.

Samuel was watching her in amusement. "I might let you take the black out for a ride one of these days," he said suddenly. "You get such a charge out of driving him."

Annie looked over at him hopefully. "I'd love to," she blurted. "It's what he was meant for. He's a pleasure horse, and I wish you'd only use him for riding!"

"Nah, Annie, this black is a race horse," he corrected, looking out at it lazily. "He's the fastest horse in the county!"

"Oh, you and your racing," Annie replied. "Why do you need to race this buggy, Samuel? It's not like there aren't other things to do. I thought the ziplining was way more fun."

"I can tell you've been talking to Aaron," Samuel said dryly. "It's your mouth, but his words."

"They're *my* words, and you know it," Annie replied tartly. "And I wish you'd stop racing, Samuel."

"Well, I can't promise that," he grinned. "At least, not today." He pointed to the road ahead of them, and to Annie's outrage, another buggy was parked off on the shoulder just ahead. She turned to him, eyes blazing.

"Is this why you brought me out here today," she demanded, "to go on another buggy race?"

"Aw, don't pretend you don't love it, Annie," Samuel told

her. "I know you do. You love going fast more than anyone I know, except me!"

The other boy looked out his window and waved to them. "Are you letting a girl drive you now, Samuel?" he gibed, and Annie scowled at him.

"Go boil your head, Andy Byler!" she called angrily, and then rounded on Samuel. "You didn't even bother to *ask* me if I wanted to do this," she fumed. "And the more I think about it, the more I think that Aaron might be right. It's stupid!"

Samuel flushed a dull red. "You were happy enough to do it the other day," he shot back. "You were as glad to win as I was!"

"Well I've changed my mind," Annie retorted. "And I don't like it that you didn't ask me what *I* wanted, before you brought me out!

"You can't go racing on this road anyway"—she gestured at the road ahead—"there are houses on it. We were out in the country the other day. This is too close in!"

Samuel pulled the reins out of her hands. "I've already given my word," he told her stubbornly. "If you don't want to go, you can wait for me here!"

"*Oh!*"

Annie pulled her mouth into a furious knot and jumped out of the cab. Then she turned back to face him, hands on hips.

"If you dump me here by the side of the road, Samuel Stauffer, you needn't to come back to look. I'll be gone, and it'll be the last time I ever get into a buggy with you!"

"I'm not dumping you, Annie," Samuel replied tautly. "You jumped out!"

And with that, he shook the reins and drove away. Annie watched in outrage as he pulled up to the other rig, and squared off to one side.

"On three!"

"One…two…*three!*"

The buggies took off with a thunderous clatter, and Annie watched in disgust as they jostled each other all the way down the road, around the corner, and out of sight.

Samuel glanced in the mirror and watched Annie's reflection get smaller and smaller. He leaned forward and gripped the reins grimly. Annie's angry eyes burned at him from the road ahead, and he blinked and shook them away. He had to have all his wits about him on a race like this one.

He shouted to the black, and it roared down the road like a whirlwind.

There was only one available shoulder on the road ahead, on the left side of the road. The right side had a deep drainage ditch, lawns and an occasional mailbox.

Samuel yanked the black over and pushed Andy Byler's rig over the berm on the left side of the road. He slapped the reins, and the black flashed ahead.

"Get up!" he yelled. "Come on!"

He surged ahead, rattling down the road like a tornado, but he could feel Andy creeping up on the left side. He pulled the black over to the left again, and laughed to see Andy jam the brakes and shoot back.

"Ha!" he yelled, "too slow!"

There was a curve at the end of the road, and Samuel drove the black toward it. He moved sharply to the left, because he was going to have to swing wide to make it at the speed he was going. He slapped the reins hard, and the black laid its ears back.

Andy was pushing again from behind, but he'd left him too little room and too little time to gain. Samuel leaned out to the left and pulled the black's head to make the turn. The buggy swung out smoothly and made the turn like the wheels were greased, and Samuel laughed out loud to see Andy's buggy tip, wobble and settle back down on the pavement with a *thud*.

The road was now a long, flat stretch with a level green shoulder on either side. There was only a few thousand feet to the finish line. Samuel shouted to the black, and it pounded the road for him. Samuel slapped the reins again. He was so close to winning, he could taste it.

But, to his horror, a white blur suddenly darted across the road ahead. A little half-naked toddler ran right out in front of the black, followed by a little girl. There was no time to stop.

Samuel yanked the black to the left as hard as he could, and the rig slid violently across the road and slammed into a stand of young trees. There was a sickening *bump*, and then a *crack*, and the sound of screaming and thrashing, just before his head hit the dash and he blacked out.

CHAPTER TWENTY-THREE

Cora Muller looked up from Naomi Zook's couch and frowned.

"What was that noise?"

She turned to look out of the window, and her face went deathly white. "*Isaac Joseph*!" she shrieked, jumping up.

"What is it?" Naomi cried, but Cora burst out the front door and went flying across the lawn. When Naomi stood up to look, to her horror, two buggies were lying smashed on the road, and there was no sign of the children who had been playing on the lawn only minutes before.

She picked up her skirts and ran out after Cora.

Naomi saw Cora's big husband intercept her on the lawn. "Stay back, Cora," he was telling her, but she crashed into his arms and thrashed there like a wild thing. "My baby!" she was screaming, "Isaac, my baby!"

"I'll find him," he was saying, "I'll go find him, Cora."

Naomi ran up, took Cora in her arms, and shot a pleading look at her own husband. "Go back to the house," he was calling.

"Where's Ruth?" she cried.

"I'll find her," he promised, and ran out to the road.

Naomi put an arm around Cora's shoulders and half-dragged her back to the house, but Cora twisted around and strained against her. Naomi prayed incoherently, and cried.

"Our Father who art in Heaven…though I walk through the valley of the…fear no evil…"

They made it as far as the porch, and Cora suddenly yanked away from her.

"Oh, no!" she was sobbing.

Naomi twisted to see Isaac Muller walking across the lawn with his little son hanging limp in his arms. Cora ran to meet him with her arms thrown wide, and Isaac put the baby tenderly into them. They bowed their heads together over him, and Isaac put his hand on Cora's shoulder.

Naomi put her own hand to her mouth, and for an instant, she couldn't see the baby at all. Cora was hunched over him, crushing her face into him, sobbing into his neck.

Then she saw the baby raise his head, and put his chubby

arms around her.

Naomi exhaled, but her relief was only for an instant. Her eyes searched anxiously for her own husband. She still couldn't see him.

But she saw Isaac Muller turn, as if someone had called him. He looked back down at his son, and put a hand on his head. Then he turned back to the road, leaving Cora to sink to her knees with the baby in her arms.

Isaac Muller ran to the nearest buggy. It was lying on its side on the road, its windows smashed and broken. The harness had snapped and the horse had run clean away.

Isaac stepped closer, and a brown-haired boy was pulling himself up off the ground. There was a cut on his head bleeding down into his eyes, and he was holding one arm oddly.

Isaac stared at him grimly. His first impulse was to pick the boy up and throttle him, but the boy's dazed expression slowly damped the fires of his anger.

"Are you all right?" he asked brusquely.

The boy nodded, and Isaac left him there without another word. He ran to the left side of the road. Another buggy had smashed into a tree, and had landed upright, but tilted over to one side.

But Isaac turned from the buggy, because nearby, a beautiful black horse lay dying on the ground. Broken limbs were scattered all around it, and one of them had pierced it like a spear. It rolled its eyes, and thrashed, and screamed in agony. A blond boy was sitting on the ground nearby, crying into his hands.

He looked up through his hair as Isaac approached, and sobbed hoarsely: "For pity's sake, give me a gun! Let me put him out of his pain!"

Isaac looked at his dark, dilated eyes. "Are you okay?"

"I don't know," the boy muttered, "and I don't care! Just give me a gun!"

"Come away from him," Isaac told him, and lifted him up by one arm. "I have a hunting gun in my rig. I'll do it. Come."

Isaac held him up by his arm, and the boy staggered across the road like a rag doll. Isaac deposited him on the Zook's lawn, and went to get his gun.

When he returned, the black was in spasm. Its muscles shivered as if with cold, and its eyes were fixed on a point far out into the trees.

Isaac felt another wave of anger. He lifted the rifle and put a clean shot between the horse's eyes. It went limp immediately.

He turned back to the house, but only got halfway across the road before he stopped, dumbstruck. Nathan Zook was kneeling in the middle of the road, weeping, holding his little daughter in his arms.

Isaac went running to him. He put the gun down and knelt on the ground beside him.

"Is she alive?" he asked urgently.

"I don't know," Nathan was sobbing. "I can't feel her heart!"

"I'll call an ambulance," Isaac muttered, and fumbled for his cell phone. "I'll come with you."

"Keep Naomi away," his friend was mumbling, "I can't let her see Ruth like this."

Isaac looked down for an instant, and grimaced in dismay. The little girl had been horribly scraped and torn on the road, and in one place, he could see the bare bones of her arm.

The operator picked up. "Nine one-one," she intoned.

Isaac came to himself. "Send an ambulance, quick, to the County Line Road," he told her. "There's been an accident. A child's been run over, another is hurt, and two boys have been injured."

"We're sending someone out now."

Isaac's eyes rolled to Ruth Zook in horrified pity. "One child is near death. *Hurry!*"

CHAPTER TWENTY-FOUR

Joseph Lapp picked up his cell phone and put it to his ear. There was a faint, agitated buzzing, audible even to his wife sitting a few feet away.

Joseph's light eyes rolled to the ceiling in an expression of instantaneous prayer.

"That's all you know?"

Katie looked up from her sewing. She had been pulling thread through a piece of fabric, but the expression on her husband's face made her hand freeze in the air.

Joseph nodded. "I'll be over as soon as I can. Call me again if you hear more."

He folded up the cell phone and turned to his wife. "There's been a horrible accident out at the County Line Road," he told her. "A racing accident. Abel Byler says that a little child got run over, a toddler, and that it may be dead."

Katie put a hand to her mouth. "Oh, Joseph! Who's out there?"

"I think, I think the Hardbargers, and the Eshes, and the Zooks," Joseph murmured, "but only the Zooks have children that young. It must be Naomi and Nathan."

Emma had been listening from the kitchen with a stricken look, but at this, she clapped her hand over her mouth.

"Oh, *Daed!*" she cried, "I was over at Aunt Cora's today, and she told me that she and Isaac were going to visit the Zooks," she cried. "She said that they were going to let Isaac Joseph play with their little daughter!"

"*Gott hilf mir!*" Katie gasped, and rolled her eyes to her husband's. "Oh, it couldn't be Isaac Joseph," she cried, "that's not possible!"

All the color drained out of Joseph's face, and for an instant he looked almost old. "I'm going over," he told them, and shrugged into his coat.

"I'm coming with you," Katie told him, but he shook his head. "I want you to stay here, Katie," he told her, but his wife met his eyes.

"I'm coming with you, or I'm following on my own, Joseph," she said, in a low voice. Joseph's shoulders sagged, and he nodded. "I don't have the time to argue with you, Katie," he told her and took her arm. He looked over his shoulder at Emma.

"Stay here, Emma, and if anyone calls, tell them that we went to the Zooks." He opened the front door, but paused on the threshold and looked back.

"And pray!"

It was late afternoon, and the sun was slanting through the trees as they set out on the road. Joseph pushed his horse as fast as it would go, and they were soon skimming down the back roads that few but the locals knew. Katie sat with her head bowed and her lips moving faintly in silent prayer, and Joseph stared at the road grimly.

Joseph turned off a narrow road and onto an even smaller back country lane. The road ran out to Silver Lake, and the County Line Road branched off to the left about two miles away.

A solitary figure walking on the road ahead made him knit his brows. He put a hand up against the glare of the westering sun.

"Katie, who is that?"

Katie opened her eyes. A slender Amish girl was walking in the distance ahead. "Why, that looks like Annie!" she marveled. "What's she doing all the way out here, alone?"

Joseph drove to meet her and pulled the horse up beside her on the grass. "Annie, what are you doing here?" he demanded.

She limped over to the buggy and raised angry eyes to his. "Samuel Stauffer took me out for a buggy ride, I *thought*," she fumed, "but after he got me out here, he said it was *really* a buggy race, and so I got out. I told him I'd rather walk home, than to let him pull a trick like that on me, and I'm never getting into his buggy again!"

Katie's mouth crumpled. "Annie, there's been an accident," she told her softly. "We don't know who was in it, yet, but two boys are hurt, and a little child may be dead. We even fear—"

Her voice broke, and she closed her eyes.

Annie's mouth fell open in dismay. "Is Samuel okay?" she cried.

"We don't know, Annie," Joseph answered grimly. "We're going now to find out. Get in, we'll take you home. But I want you to stay in the buggy, when we get to the Zook's."

Annie climbed quickly into the back seat of her uncle's buggy and curled up into a frightened ball of confusion. Fear surged up like a cold, black wave and smothered her anger beneath it. She closed her eyes, imagining Samuel lying on the road somewhere unconscious, bleeding, or with broken bones.

This couldn't be real, surely it wasn't real.

She'd left Samuel not even an hour before, and he'd been fine. He would surely come driving up any minute now, with a wink and a grin, to tell her that the black had won again, and wheedle her to ride back home with him.

Not *this*.

And what about the other boy, and the little child? Grief rose up in Annie's chest and stuck in her throat like a bone that would not be swallowed.

What if the little child died, and it was Samuel's fault?

It couldn't happen, that was all. It just *couldn't*.

A soft touch on her head made Annie look up. Her Aunt Katie was looking at her with tears in her eyes, and Annie almost burst out crying. But she made herself swallow it.

She hated to cry, and she wasn't going to cry.

Because if she cried, it would all be real, and it wasn't, couldn't be real.

Annie turned her face away, squeezed her eyes together and prayed harder than she'd ever prayed in her life.

Oh, Jesus, please let everything be all right. Please, please don't let the child die, or-or the other boy, and let Samuel—she pulled her mouth down—*don't let Samuel be hurt, Jesus, please, please!*

Joseph whipped up the horse again, and the buggy went rushing down the road again. But to Annie's dismay, as they got closer, they could hear the sounds of a dispatch radio over a loudspeaker, and a huge engine running.

Joseph pulled the horse to the left, and they turned at last onto County Line Road. They all strained forward, scanning the road anxiously. The scene that met their eyes was one of chaos.

There was a fire engine and two ambulances on the road outside the Zook's house. They were just in time to see a couple of paramedics lift a stretcher into the back of one of the ambulances. Nathan Zook climbed into the passenger seat and the paramedics slammed the door. The lights on the ambulance began to flash, and it roared off down the road with its sirens wailing.

Their horse whinnied in fright and tried to rear up, and Joseph had to yank back hard on the reins. He jumped out of the cab, led the horse to the side of the road, and put blinders over its eyes.

Annie looked out ahead.

A young woman was standing in the middle of the yard, crying, and some other women were standing around her, comforting her. Cora Muller was sitting on the porch, crying, and cradling Isaac Joseph in her arms.

Andy Byler was lying flat in the middle of the road, and two paramedics were strapping him onto a board. They already had him in a neck brace.

And across the street from the house, and far distant from the others, Samuel Stauffer was sitting on the side of the road with his head bowed and his hands hanging limply over his knees.

"*Annie!*" Joseph called, but it was too late.

Annie had already jumped down from the buggy and was running down the road like a mad thing.

CHAPTER TWENTY-FIVE

"Samuel!"

Samuel looked up and suddenly twisted away.

"Get away from me, Annie!"

Annie came to a dead stop in the middle of the road. She looked down at him, wide-eyed and panting.

"I said get away*!*" he screamed, and threw a pebble at her.

Annie came ahead, and knelt down on the ground beside him. "Are you okay, Samuel?" she whispered urgently.

He looked resolutely away from her, and shook his head. "Does it *look* like I'm okay?" he cried, staring off into the distance. "What are you doing here, anyway?"

Annie's anxious eyes scanned his body. She leaned in and took his hand, but Samuel pushed her away.

"Get away from me, Annie!"

"No."

Samuel turned around, and his face was red and tear-streaked. His eyes were puffy, almost swollen closed, but the look of anguish in them twisted something in Annie's chest.

"Is this what you came to see?" he cried, gesturing to his face. "Then take a good look! I killed the black, Annie! It's dead! I ran over a kid, and it's probably dead, too! If you've come to say *I told you so*, then say it and get out!"

Annie shook her head. Her mouth twisted in grief, and she couldn't trust herself not to burst out crying; but she did what she could still do.

She reached out without a word, and took Samuel in her arms. And to her relief, this time he didn't push her away.

Annie put a hand on the back of his head, and pressed her cheek gently to his. For an instant his body was tense and trembling. Then he dropped his head on her shoulder and sobbed like a child.

Annie looked up into the blurry sky and rocked Samuel in her arms. And the only thought in her mind was, *thank you.*

Joseph stared out at his niece in exasperation. Annie was crouching on the ground, holding Samuel Stauffer in her arms. Her father's angry face appeared to him, but Katie called:

"Let her go, Joseph. Naomi and Cora need us more right

now!"

She climbed down out of the buggy and together they hurried across the lawn to where Cora was sitting on the Zook's porch steps. Cora looked up and saw them coming, and she broke out sobbing, stood up, and held out her arms.

Katie flew into them and hugged her tight; but Joseph grabbed Isaac Joseph up in his arms and searched him with his fingers. He picked up the baby's hands, felt of his ribs and checked his legs.

"Oh, Katie, I only looked away for a *second*!" Cora was sobbing. "Only a second and my baby was gone!" She put her face in her hands. "It's a *miracle* that our baby's alive. Isaac says that Naomi's little girl might not make it. The buggy missed Isaac Joseph, but little Ruth was run over!"

"*Hush, hush*," Katie soothed, and looked over at Joseph. "Is the baby all right?"

Cora sobbed again and caressed the baby's cheek. "He's got scratch marks, and he's scared, but we think he's okay. The paramedics want to take him to the hospital, but I won't let strangers take my baby away!"

At this, Joseph looked up from his inspection. "Where's Isaac?"

"He's talking to them now," Cora quavered, wiping her eyes.

Joseph handed the baby back to Cora, and she cradled him hungrily in her arms. Katie sat down on the steps with her, and put her arm around Cora's shoulders as Joseph crossed the lawn.

He walked over to the group of women surrounding Naomi Zook, and they looked up.

"I'm so sorry, Naomi," he said softly. "I saw Nathan leave in the ambulance. We will all be praying for Ruthie, and I'm about to go to the hospital. I'll be there with them."

She nodded, and Joseph turned away to look for Isaac.

He found him in the middle of the road, listening to a pair of paramedics. As he approached, one of the paramedics was saying: "…needs to be checked at the hospital, to be sure he's okay. It's your decision, but your baby could show up with a problem tonight, or a few days from now, if you don't do it."

Isaac looked up, and relief flooded his face. Joseph reached out and put a reassuring arm on his shoulder.

"Cora says she doesn't want you to take Isaac Joseph to the hospital," he murmured, and Isaac nodded. He looked back toward the house.

"I don't want to upset Cora any more than she has been," he replied, in a low voice. "It might not be good for the baby."

"You can both come with us, if you want to," the paramedic put in, and Joseph looked at Isaac with sympathetic eyes.

"Take the baby to the hospital, Isaac," he said. "I'm not telling you as your brother-in-law. I'm telling you as your bishop. I'll square it with Cora.

"You have to make sure Isaac Joseph is all right."

Isaac's eyes were troubled, but he nodded, and together they walked back to the house.

Cora raised her eyes once, and read their intent right off her husband's face.

"No, no, Isaac!" she cried, and grabbed the baby close. "No, I'm not going to let you take him!"

Isaac sat down on the steps in front of her and pled with his eyes. "Cora, we have to let him be checked. It's for his good."

Cora's mouth turned down like a child's. "He'll be so scared," she objected. "It's a strange place, filled with strange people. My poor little boy!"

"I'll go with Isaac," Joseph put in softly. "I'll go with him, Cora. The baby won't be scared. He'll have his Daed and his Uncle Joes right there with him. It will be all right."

Katie turned to look at her, and Cora weakened. "If the baby goes, I want to go too," she said at last, but Isaac shook his head.

"You need to go home and rest, Cora," he told her. "We have two babies now, and you have to think about the least one. I'll bring Isaac Joseph back safe and sound."

He put his big hands out for the baby, and Cora looked dangerously close to another bout of tears; she kissed the baby's cheek and hesitated, but finally handed him reluctantly over to Isaac.

Isaac took the baby gently in his arms, and squeezed Cora's hand. "Go home, Cora," he told her, "and try to rest. They may not keep us long. I'll bring the baby back as soon as they tell us it's safe."

Joseph looked down at Katie. "Take Cora home, Katie. And Annie, too. It's getting late. I'll be back as soon as I can, but I may stay the night at the hospital."

Katie looked sympathetically at her husband, but nodded, and the two of them left.

But Joseph made a short detour across the lawn and down the road a few hundred yards.

Annie looked up at her uncle's approach, and the look on his usually patient face told her that the news wasn't going to be good. She raised pleading eyes to his, but didn't dare to open her mouth.

He looked way too angry.

Joseph approached grimly, and Annie helped Samuel to stand up to meet him. Samuel looked up through his hair, breathing hard.

"Samuel Stauffer," Joseph said quietly, "you were warned. I stood in the pulpit and warned all of you, that if no one came forward to confess, it would go hard when the truth came out. Well, now it *has*." He turned and gestured toward the scene of chaos behind them, and Samuel lowered his head.

"I'm going to the hospital tonight to make sure my little nephew doesn't have hidden injuries, and to pray that Ruthie Zook survives. I recommend that you do the same."

He stopped and took a deep breath, and looked up at the sky.

"I know that none of you have yet joined the church. I can't put you under the *bann*, as much as you might deserve it! But you disobeyed willfully, and after you'd been warned, and this is the result. You need to learn that actions have consequences!

"Here is your chance to show your repentance, Samuel Stauffer," he went on grimly. "You will go to Nathan and Naomi Zook and beg their forgiveness of your carelessness and pride. You will go to the hospital to see their daughter. You will do whatever you can to help them through this terrible time. That will give you a chance to think about what you've done, and to repent. And when Andrew Byler heals, he will do it, too. Maybe when you boys see the cost of your foolishness, you'll understand that we have rules for a reason!"

His eyes turned to Annie, and she shrank under the look in them.

"And *you*, Annie Miller – you knew this was going on and

yet you said nothing to anyone. I can't command you to repent, but I expect you to. Next Sunday I want you to stand up in front of the congregation and do what you should have done at first – confess your sin, and repent!"

Then, with one last fiery look, he turned and walked down the road to where Isaac Muller's buggy was waiting and climbed inside. The buggy clattered down the road, leaving them to stare after it in dismay.

Annie looked over at the house and saw Katie take Cora's arm and lead her across the lawn toward the buggy.

She turned to Samuel and said urgently: "Go with the paramedics, Samuel. Let them check you. I have some money in my bag, and you can use it to get a cab home."

Samuel looked at her out of the corner of his eye. "Go home, Annie," he murmured darkly, and then sputtered and broke out into wild laughter. *"Leave me alone!"*

Annie looked up to see Katie and Cora climbing into her uncle's buggy. "Annie! Come with us."

When she hesitated, she was surprised to hear her gentle aunt add:

"Now!"

Annie gave Samuel one long, last look, and then retreated. But when Katie shook the reins, and the buggy pulled away, Annie looked back at Samuel until the curve of the road hid him from sight.

Earlier that day, the thought of Samuel Stauffer having to walk home would've seemed like justice. But now, riding home in the back seat of her uncle's buggy, strict justice didn't seem quite so urgent.

No one was looking at her, and no one asked her any questions, so Annie took advantage of her temporary invisibility. She curled her knees up to her chest, bowed her head on them, and indulged her feelings at last.

CHAPTER TWENTY-SIX

Joseph Lapp climbed out of Isaac Muller's buggy at two o' clock the next morning. He waved as the buggy pulled away, trudged wearily across the dark lawn, and unlocked the front door of his house.

The kitchen and living room were dark, but when he went to the refrigerator, he saw that Katie had made a plate and a cup of coffee for him. He sighed gratefully and sat down at the table to eat them.

After a few minutes, a yellow light bloomed at the top of the stairs, and Katie padded down silently, barefoot and in her nightgown. She was carrying a kerosene lamp.

She set it down on the table and sat down beside her husband. She put a hand on his shoulder and rubbed his back.

"How's Ruthie?"

Joseph turned weary eyes to hers. "She's in intensive care.

They say it could go either way. We can only pray."

Katie's mouth drooped. "What about Isaac Joseph?"

"They said that there's no sign of any internal injuries. God was merciful to us."

Katie closed her eyes and leaned her brow against her husband's. She nodded.

"Cora's upstairs sleeping. I thought it would be better for her to spend the night here," she told him. "Annie's here too. I called Mose and told him that she's here with us, but I didn't tell him what happened. I thought that news was best left for morning."

"He'll probably hear of it by then, anyway," Joseph muttered, and pulled his knobby hands over his face. "I don't know what I'm going to do, Katie. I told Samuel and Andrew to repent and make amends for their part in this, but this thing could go far beyond that.

"Of course, Nathan and Naomi won't press charges. But I overheard one of the nurses say that if Ruthie died, the state could bring charges of involuntary manslaughter against Samuel and Andrew. She said that they could go to jail for five years."

Katie's eyes widened. "Oh, Joseph," she groaned.

"If it comes to that, the elders could talk to a lawyer. I've heard that sometimes they go easier on a boy if it's his first offense, or if he's sorry. And there were no signs that they'd been drinking – thank God!"

"Do you think Andrew and Samuel *are* sorry?" Katie worried aloud.

"Yes. I think they both are. But Samuel—" he shook his head. "He's wild, Katie. He worries me. There's a streak of something in him, something destructive. Or at least, that's my fear.

"Lots of boys get into a scrape now and then," he sighed, "but Samuel seems to court trouble. I think there's a part of him that enjoys it. Oh, I don't say that he caused this accident on purpose. But he seems to love living right on the edge."

"And Annie's attracted to that," Katie murmured, half to herself. She leaned against her husband's back and stared into the darkness. "If Samuel goes to jail, Annie will be heartbroken."

"Annie won't be the only one," Joseph answered sadly. He was silent for awhile, and then added: "I should've stepped in when you told me that Annie looked guilty at church the other day. I should've gotten the truth out of her. It would've been easy, and it might have prevented all this."

"Don't blame yourself," Katie murmured and kissed him. "And don't be too sure. Annie is very loyal to her friends. Too loyal, maybe. She probably wouldn't have told you what she knew."

"You think Annie would hide the truth from me, from her bishop? That's rebellion, Katie," he said softly.

"I suppose," she breathed, and shook her head. "But if so, it would be because she was trying to protect someone she loved.

"I was wrong, Joseph. I assumed that Annie was seeing Aaron Graber, but it was Samuel. See what comes of being wrong!"

Her husband reached around behind her, and pulled her to his chest. "You can't stop them from seeing each other, if they're really determined to do it," he whispered into her ear. "Isn't that what you told me once?"

"Yes. But *that* turned out all right, and I don't think this is going to," Katie mourned.

"Enough thinking, and worrying," Joseph said, and pulled Katie to her feet. He picked up the kerosene lamp in one hand, and put the other arm around his wife. "Come to bed, and let's get some rest. We'll need it, if we're going to do all that must be done in the morning."

Katie allowed herself to be drawn, and they slowly climbed the stairs to their bedroom. But as they turned the corner and paused in front of the door, a slight motion made Katie turn her head.

She was just in time to see the door to Annie's room slip closed.

.

CHAPTER TWENTY-SEVEN

The next Sunday, Annie sat alone on a bench facing the whole church congregation; her mouth was dry, eyes wide, and hands shaking. Her uncle stood at her side, staring at her meaningfully.

Joseph stood in front of the congregation and gave the assembled worshippers an update on the Zooks. "I spoke to Nathan this morning," he announced, "and he asks for our prayers. Ruthie is still in the ICU, in critical condition."

There were nods and murmured prayers from different corners of the room, and Joseph went on: "Several youngie from our church were involved in this accident, and I have encouraged them all to confess their sin and repent.

"Annie Miller is here this morning to confess her *fehla*," Joseph intoned solemnly. "She knew that Samuel Stauffer, and some other boys, were racing their buggies on the roads in a dangerous way. She did not share this information with me voluntarily; she did not share it when I asked for those who knew of it, to confess it."

Annie looked out across the rows of faces in Mark Fisher's barn. Her Daed sat looking at her, his eyes dark with equal parts disappointment and concern; Tim was goggling at her, no doubt thanking his lucky stars that he hadn't fallen into the net; and her Aunt Katie and Cousin Emma were looking at her with grave sympathy. Annie couldn't bring herself to meet Cora Muller's eyes, and when she looked beyond, her glance got tangled up on the Yoder sisters. Their faces expressed a grim approval of her confession, and Annie moved her eyes back to the men's benches.

David Ropp was staring at her in complete stillness, and Annie wondered briefly if he was sleeping with his eyes open, because he was able to do it. And then her glance brushed across Aaron Graber's face.

To Annie, who knew his every mood, his face may as well have been tattooed with the words, *I'm dying*. He was looking down at the floor, frowning. His shoulders were stiff, his arms rigid at his side.

But even so, she wasn't prepared for him to stand up and announce:

"I knew it, too."

An audible gasp rippled through the congregation, and Joseph frowned.

"Do you want to make a confession too, Aaron?"

Aaron nodded, and Joseph motioned for him to come forward.

Aaron walked to the front of the room and sat down on the bench beside Annie, his eyes glued to the floor. Annie was so flustered that she stared at her uncle in blank incomprehension when he asked, "Annie, do you have something to say?"

But then the words came back to her, and she nodded. She took a deep breath and recited the words that were customary for confessing *fehla*: "I want to confess that I have failed..." she quavered.

Joseph waited for her to finish her recitation, and nodded to Aaron. "Aaron, what do you have to say?"

He looked out across the congregation, and echoed the same words solemnly.

Joseph turned to face them. "Are you, Annie, and you, Aaron, willing to change your ways, and to put the good of *all* the people above your own desire to please a friend?"

Annie dropped her glance to the floor and muttered *Yes*; but on the inside, she was wondering if she'd have the strength, if she was tempted again. Samuel hadn't come to church, but Annie couldn't stop thinking about him, worrying about him.

She couldn't help wondering where he was, and what he was doing.

Joseph raised his hand and called for prayer, and the room

went silent for several long minutes. Then the meeting broke up at last, and Annie felt almost giddy with relief that it was over. Since neither she nor Aaron were members of the church, their confession was considered voluntary, and there was no mention of any further repercussions.

But Annie was still keenly conscious of having submitted to a very public community spanking. The fact that Aaron had volunteered to share it with her both surprised her and took away what little was left of her anger toward him.

After the church lunch was over, she found him sitting on a bench outside the Fisher's barn.

"Hi."

"Hi, Annie. Sit down." He patted the bench invitingly, and Annie sat down next to him. He added nothing else, and it was a long time before she found the courage to say: "I'm sorry, Aaron. I was mean to you before, and you didn't deserve it."

He shrugged, and glanced off across Mark Fisher's bean field. "I wasn't mad. I understood."

Annie looked down at her hands. "You were right. I wish I'd seen it earlier. I wish…Samuel had seen it."

Aaron nodded, but refused to rub it in – for which Annie was grateful, because he could have.

He fell silent again, and finally added, "I guess I might have gone about it better," he confessed. "And my motives weren't everything they should have been."

Annie glanced at him in surprise.

"It was true that I saw an accident coming, and that I was trying to keep it from happening.

"But it was also true that I was jealous of Samuel, Annie."

Annie stared at him, open-mouthed. She could scarcely credit her ears, but Aaron wasn't laughing.

He turned to her, and his eyes were serious. "I was jealous because you were spending time with him, and not with me."

Annie closed her eyes and shook her head, as if that would help her process what he'd said. And because she didn't know what to say, she took refuge in the past.

"But I've always spent time with you," she teased, with a crooked smile.

But he left her no out. "No, Annie. I mean, I want to *go out* with you. I want to court you."

Annie felt herself going red to the ends of her hair, and she looked down quickly. Her mind and her heart were full of Samuel. Her heart was wrung with pity for him, she dreamed of him at night.

But she wasn't sure that they'd ever go out again. Samuel had changed. He'd screamed at her, told her to go away.

Aaron's eyes were pleading with her against his will, and

her heart broke when she thought of hurting him.

And because she could think of nothing else to say, she heard herself saying: "I've been seeing Samuel, Aaron. But if that's all right with you, I-I could go out with you. If you want that."

Aaron smiled sadly and took her hand. "Yeah, Annie. I want that," he replied softly, and leaned over and kissed her.

Annie received his lips with wonder. Because, to her chagrin, they, *too*, were soft and warm.

When Aaron pulled back, he smiled down at her. "Don't look so guilty, Annie. I know I'm not your first choice. But maybe, one day I'll be your *last* one."

And then he kissed her again.

Annie gave herself up to it, but confusion roiled her mind. She could only hope that, somehow, she could find the strength to help Samuel, avoid hurting Aaron, and understand herself.

Because she had the uneasy feeling that the three of them were rushing toward yet another terrible collision.

THE END.

THANK YOU FOR READING!

And thank you for supporting me as an independent author. I hope you enjoyed reading this as much as I loved writing it! If so, I hope you also enjoy the sample in the next chapter of my other work.

Lastly, if you enjoyed this book and want to continue to support my writing, please leave me a review to let everyone know what you thought of my work. It's the best thing you can do to keep indie authors like me writing. (And if you find something in the book that – YIKES – makes you think it deserves less than 5-stars, drop me a line at gr8godis76@gmail.com and I'll fix it if I can.)

All the best,

RUTH PRICE

LANCASTER COUNTY SECOND CHANCES

When an Amish widow and widower, against all odds, begin to fall in love, will they have the faith to risk their hearts a second time?

After Katie Fisher's husband and young son are killed in a house fire, the young Amish widow returns to her parents' home broken-hearted with her faith in shambles. Katie can never imagine herself marrying again. But when 31-year-old Amish widower, Joseph Lapp, comes to Katie's district church service looking to hire an honest woman to help him take care of his three active, rambunctious children, Katie takes the plunge and accepts the position. Katie quickly finds herself falling in love with Joseph's children, and though Katie and Joseph cannot spend time together unsupervised due to the strict tenants of their Ordnung, the widow and widower find themselves growing closer in spirit as well. But when a new tragedy threatens the fragile future Katie and Joseph have begun to build, will the couple have the faith to risk a second chance at love?

CHAPTER ONE

Katie Olsen looked out the kitchen window. The sun was just coming up, and everyone but her *mamm* and younger sister were already out in the fields. It was spring, and the rising sun spread its beams over soft brown earth, ready for planting. The landscape was the same as she remembered. The gentle hills of her Lancaster County home seemed to be forever rolling away to the horizon. It had always been a comforting view.

She picked at the white cotton tablecloth with her fingers. It was the same familiar table cloth she had used as a child – the hand sewn border, the faint stain from the strawberry accident, the little uneven nubs that she had loved to rub with her fingers.

This plain white farmhouse still looked just the same as it had when she was six years old. The massive gray barn had seemed endless then, and it still looked huge. The freshly-tilled earth would soon be filled with movement and color and sound.

This farm had been her home. She had felt so comfortable in it, as if she herself had been a young plant springing up from her *daed*'s fields. She had grown from this soil, like the oak trees overshadowing the house. Like her mamm's roses. Like the wheat that swayed and whispered secrets to the lavender twilight. Once, her world had been as safe and predictable as bud and bloom and harvest. It had seemed to her that nothing would ever change.

But everything had changed. She was 26 now. The familiar white farmhouse wasn't her home any longer. It was her parents' home.

The tablecloth, the house, the barn, the oak trees, and even the rolling hills, all of them belonged to the child she had been, not the young woman she had become.

For the past three months, she had been an increasingly uncomfortable guest in her parents' home.

Maybe even a burden.

Of course, her mamm and daed would never put it that way. And she did her best to help them around the house and with her little sister and brother.

But still.

Katie's fingertip raised the corner of a paper lying underneath her breakfast plate. Her mamm had "forgotten" it there this morning.

It was an Amish advertising circular. The headline read: Young Widowed Men Interested in Remarriage.

A cheerful voice interrupted Katie's thoughts.

"Why such a sad face, Katze?"

Katie pulled her lips into a smile and turned to face her 10-

year-old sister, Bett.

"No sad face for you, Bett." She pulled her blonde giggle box of a sister into her arms and smiled. "Come, I will help you with your chores."

They walked out to the chicken coop and roused the hens. Katie had always liked gathering eggs – the sleepy, blinking hens, the feel of their soft feathers, the warm, smooth eggs.

Bett was skipping in her joy. "I'm glad you're back, Katze," she was saying, calling Katie by the nickname everyone in her family used. Bett's blue eyes were full of affection.

Katie stopped gathering eggs momentarily. She bit her lip. She wished she could say, I am glad to be back, but that would have been a lie, and she already had too many sins on her soul.

"I'm glad you are pleased," was what she said.

"Everyone is pleased," Bett nattered on. "Last Sunday I heard Mr. Hershberger say that you have a pleasing countenance and that you are a diligent worker. And Mr. Beiler said that he's glad you're back, and that it's a good thing."

Bett dug a toe into the dirt and smiled shyly up at Katie.

"I think they like you," she added, in a conspiratorial tone.

Katie stifled an impatient exclamation. Mr. Hershberger was 20 years her elder. He was bald and fat and had an ungovernable temper. And Mr. Beiler was 70 if he was a day and as shriveled as a stick. The last thing in the world she wanted was to attract the attention of men like Mr. Hershberger and Mr. Beiler.

Or, really, the attention of any man.

She closed her eyes and counted slowly to ten before saying, "I think that's all for now, Bett. Let's take these back."

Bett giggled and skipped along beside her. "I can't wait until I'm your age, Katze," she confided, "and all the men are asking after me."

Katie said nothing in reply, but she was wishing with all her soul that she could somehow revert to her sister's age and once again be a freckled, laughing child.

***

At dinner that night, the table was laden with baked bread and butter, beans and bacon, ham, baked potatoes, apple pie topped with cheese. It was good, solid farmhouse cooking, some of which Katie had made herself, but she had no appetite.

Katie's mamm shot her husband a glance. He straightened in his chair and cleared his throat.

"Are you feeling ill, Katze?" he rumbled.

"No, Daed," she replied.

"Eat, then."

She dutifully picked up a forkful of potatoes and put it into her mouth.

Katie retreated to bed immediately after dinner, pleading a throbbing head. Her parents had put her in her old bedroom. It still looked much the same as it had – the bare wooden floor, the plain single bed next to the big window overlooking the fields, the same starburst quilt that her grandmother had made for her when she born, with its red, blue, and green.

Even her old toys were still there – the old cotton doll and the stuffed bear that she had worn to shreds, all still lying at the bottom of the quilt chest at the foot of her bed.

There was the prayer book she had used as a child, still with her childish scrawls inside.

The old bedroom should have been a reassuring haven, but for Katie, it was oddly jarring – a reminder of what she wasn't anymore, and could never be again.

Just as she had always done, she knelt down beside the bed for her evening prayers. As a child, it had been easy and natural for her to pray to God. She had felt His presence everywhere. But tonight, she found no words to say. Now, she didn't feel His presence at all.

She had not felt His presence for months. Sometimes, in her darkest moments, she even feared that God had…

The sound of a soft knock at Katie's bedroom door ended her devotions. Katie rose and opened the door to find her mamm standing outside. The candlelight touched her braided brown hair with gold.

"May I come in?"

"Of course." Katie sat down on the bed and patted the space beside her. Katie's mamm sat down quickly and put an arm around her. Her eyes looked worried.

"I shouldn't have left that advertisement on the table. I think I've upset you," she said softly. "I'm sorry. I didn't mean to."

"You have a right," Katie replied, looking down.

"It's not about our rights," her mamm corrected quickly. "Your daed and I, we just want to see you smile again. To come back again, just a little bit." She smoothed a tendril of Katie's soft brown hair back from her face. "It was too soon, maybe."

"You're not the only ones," Katie told her, with an unhappy grimace. "Bett told me today that Mr. Hershberger and Mr. Beiler were asking after me," Katie added, wrinkling her nose.

Her mamm burst out laughing and hugged her close. "Then I don't blame you for picking at your food tonight." She smiled. "It would trouble me, too."

Katie smiled in spite of herself, and her mamm laughed again. "There," she said tenderly, lifting Katie's chin. "That's what I was looking for. My Katze."

Suddenly everything that had happened, everything that she had lost, welled up in Katie's heart. "Oh, Mamm!" she cried, and sobbed as her mamm made soothing noises and rocked her back and forth like a child.

CHAPTER TWO

The next morning, Katie was up long before dawn and long before anyone else was awake. She dressed by the light of a single candle and went down to the empty kitchen. She put a piece of cheese between two slices of bread, wrapped it in a handkerchief, and put it in a bag.

She started a fire in the fireplace to make the house warm, put on her own coat, and went outside.

The predawn dark was still very damp and cold. A thick fog covered everything. Karl, her daed's old collie, was curled up in a box on the porch. He opened one eye and mustered a few thumps of his tail in greeting.

Katie bent down and ruffled his fur, then walked to the barn. Her old blue bicycle was still in the corner. She walked it out into the yard, adjusted the bag around the handlebars, and pushed off into the fog.

The beautiful pastures of Lancaster County slowly rolled

past. At first, in the dark, she knew them by the sweet smell of freshly-turned earth, the faint sound of dogs barking far away, the lowing of a cow. Then the sky began to lighten, and the fog faded to reveal big, rolling hills, which, though dark brown now, would soon be alive with fresh green. Katie inhaled deeply. She loved the scent of freshly turned earth, of dew, of new things stirring in the grass.

She pedaled past the Iverson farm, the Johansen farm, the Muller farm. Each field conjured up faces and names from the past. Most of the boys had been blonde, gangly, and tall. A few had hinted that they might like to court with her. She almost smiled, remembering John Muller and his shy calf eyes.

Of course, they hadn't ended up together. She had left home five years ago and her parents told her that John hadn't shown interest in anyone else for a good two years. That is, until Laura Pedersen grew up and caught his eye.

A sudden pain in her shoulder made Katie grimace and slow her pace.

When she was Bett's age, Katie could have arrived in town within 30 minutes. But it was becoming clear that this time, it would take her twice that, if not longer. It wasn't the fog that hindered her – she knew every pebble in those well-worn roads. She could have ridden them with her eyes closed.

It was her shoulder. The damp made it ache, and she had to go slowly to avoid pulling it. Her bandages had only come off a week before, and she couldn't bear the thought of facing another doctor.

She closed her eyes and let the bicycle bounce freely down a long, straight slope. She tried to shut it out, but even this small reminder made her peaceful thoughts drift away like the morning mists.

It made the doctor's face come back again, as it had been coming back every day for the last three months.

"I'm sorry," he was saying, and put a hand on her arm. "Is there anything you'd like us to do?"

She heard herself screaming, *Gott im Himmel*!

She put a hand to her mouth, and momentarily the handlebars left her control. The bicycle bounced dangerously off a rock and she had to hit the brakes to keep the bicycle from crashing.

Gott...

The bicycle skidded to a stop, and Katie dug her heels into the gravel to keep herself from falling over. She could feel herself trembling. She tried again to pray, to plead, to feel something, but there was nothing.

Maybe she should never have left. Maybe God had meant her to stay here, to marry John Muller.

She must not have done God's will. Because surely, if she had done it, her life wouldn't have gone so horribly wrong.

God must be angry with her, so terribly…

Katie closed her eyes and stood very still, feeling the muffled pounding of her heart. Minutes passed. A door closed somewhere in the distance, a man's voice issued a short, sharp command, and a dog barked.

God did not strike her dead. The world did not end.

She put a hand to her eyes and pushed off again.

***

"*Guten morgen*, Katie!"

It wasn't hard for Katie to muster a smile for Elie Meissen. Elie's face was as plump and red as a ripe apple, and it was always smiling. Katie had never seen her in a bad mood, but if Elie had a fault, it was that she had the longest tongue in three counties. Elie loved to get news, and she loved even more to report it.

"Guten morgen, Elie Meissen."

The Meissens ran a store in town and made their living mainly off of the sale of quilts, furniture, and other handmade crafts to tourists.

Elie tilted her head to one side, like a bird. "What brings you to town, Katie?"

"I'm looking for a job," Katie replied. "I need work, and was wondering who might need help."

Elie's bright eyes sparkled with this new intelligence. "Ah! I wish we could help you, but we already have three women who make quilts." She put a finger to her lips. "Maybe I can ask around for you."

She waved Katie around to the back of the counter. "So you came on your bicycle? That's a fair way from your farm. Have you had your breakfast?"

Katie shrugged. "I have bread and cheese."

"Bah," Elie laughed. "Come back to the office and have pie and coffee."

Elie led the way to a small office with one wooden table and three chairs. There was a small counter on one wall, and it was covered with kitchen clutter. Elie pulled out a chair for Katie and poured a cup of steaming hot coffee. "Take a piece of pie. It's coconut cream from last night. So good." Elie put a plate on the table and licked her thumb.

Katie didn't feel especially hungry, but took a few bites to be polite. The pie was very good – rich and creamy and indulgent.

"I'm so glad you're back," Elie confided, pulling up a chair. "So much has happened since you left. Let me catch you up."

Katie stifled a sigh and braced herself. Elie was never happy until she had told all she knew. Or thought she knew.

"Terese Johansen spent *rumspringa* in Philadelphia running

wild with the English, they say. She has decided to leave altogether and become a Presbyterian. Her parents are prostrated, I can tell you."

Katie was tempted to offer a tentative rebuke for Elie's gossip, but thought better of it. She was grateful that Elie was sharing news rather than asking painful questions.

Katie's annoyance softened. She was also sure that Elie's unusual forbearance was not accidental. Given Elie's love of gossip, her restraint on that point was an act of grace. Katie sipped her coffee and said nothing.

"And did you know that Martin Hoffer is the new bishop after old David Zurich died? Remember how we almost used to go to sleep during services?" She giggled. "Well, not anymore! No one can have any peace during his sermons, let alone sleep! He's the strictest bishop anyone can remember. So stern!" Her cheerful face grew scrunched up momentarily as she took a sip of coffee. "It gives me heartburn."

Katie's conscience stirred again, and again she squelched it.

"Oh!" Elie fanned her face. "And there's another newcomer besides you! Of course, you're not new, and he is, but you know what I mean. It's a widower with four *kinner*, a man named Joseph Lapp. He's from the next county. Quite good looking, so I hear. Tall. A little peaked, though."

Katie stirred uncomfortably, and Elie nattered on. "Of course, every woman in the county who has a grown daughter has set her cap for him. Though he's a little old for a girl."

A sudden ringing from the shop announced the arrival of a customer. Katie breathed a sigh of relief as Elie jumped up and finally tended to her own business.

Or almost tended to it. She could just hear the sound of a woman's voice and Elie's voice in reply. After the initial greetings, their voices lowered, but not before Katie heard the words, "Oh, the poor thing."

She sighed, shook out her skirt, and rose to leave.

CHAPTER THREE

That evening after dinner Katie went to bed early again. She undressed by the light of a candle, peeling off the plain blue dress and black stockings. She stood in front of the mirror. The sad young woman who looked back at her had soft, wavy brown hair, large, earnest green eyes, and a body that her mamm had once told her was "womanly."

Except for the stain. And now, the scar.

It was vain, and wrong, but she couldn't resist running her finger over the scar on her shoulder. Her skin was still tender from the surgery. The angry red color had faded, and the doctor had promised that it would continue to fade until it could hardly be seen. But at three months out, a faint splotch was still there, still visible, though barely, in the dim light.

The stain had been the size of a dinner plate. Its outline had been ragged and ugly. It had looked as if her right shoulder had been splashed with red wine. The purple birthmark had been her secret shame, and also her secret vanity. It had covered three inches of her upper arm, the right side of her neck, and two inches of her back.

She had hated it all her life, but her parents had told her that God loved her, and that they loved her, and that it made no difference – that it was vain to be concerned about things that did not endanger her health.

But in her vanity, she had chosen to have the hated mark removed anyway.

Katie knelt by the bed and clasped her hands. She tried to pray the prayers she had learned as a child, to be pious and meek, but something in her convulsed, and her grief suddenly came spilling out.

Oh, God, was it this? Was this why? So much, only for this?

Why not me, then?

The only reply was the sound of the candle sizzling as it wept its small tears. Katie searched her heart for any answer, any sense of God's nearness, any comfort.

Oh, God, where are you?

There was no sound, no spark of feeling. Nothing.

Sobs welled up in her throat, and her head drooped over the bed. She stopped trying to pray. It was useless. And she was too tired to spend another night with her hands over her face. She rose, blew out the candle, and slipped under the covers.

Katie was exhausted, and sleep came quickly. She felt as if her body was falling into some measureless depth, down into some infinity of sleep. Waves of unconsciousness closed over her, pushing her further and further down.

"Katze."

She turned her head and murmured softly...

THANK YOU FOR READING!

And thank you for supporting me as an independent author. I hope you enjoyed reading this as much as I loved writing it!

If so, look for this book in eBook or Paperback format at your favorite online book distributors. Also, when a series is complete, we usually put out a discounted collection. If you'd rather read the entire series at once and save a few bucks doing it, we recommend looking for the collection.

Lastly, if you enjoyed this book and want to continue to support my writing, please leave me a review to let everyone know what you thought of my work. It's the best thing you can do to keep indie authors like me writing. (And if you find something in the book that – YIKES – makes you think it deserves less than 5-stars, drop me a line at gr8godis76@gmail.com and I'll fix it if I can.)

All the best,

RUTH PRICE

ABOUT THE AUTHOR

Ruth Price is a Pennsylvania native and devoted mother of four. After her youngest set off for college, she decided it was time to pursue her childhood dream to become a fiction writer. Drawing inspiration from her faith, her husband and love of her life Harold, and deep interest in Amish culture that stemmed from a childhood summer spent with her family on a Lancaster farm, Ruth began to pen the stories that had always jabbered away in her mind. Ruth believes that art at its best channels a higher good, and while she doesn't always reach that ideal, she hopes that her readers are entertained and inspired by her stories.